MW01171288

BOOKS BY A T VEATCH

City of Thicket

Born in Silver

Divided by Metal

Tome of the Resewn

CITY
OF
THICKET

a t veatch

This is a work of fiction. All the characters and events portrayed in this book are fictitious, and any resemblance to real people or events is purely coincidental.

CITY OF THICKET

Cover art by A T Veatch

An Arkermin Project Book

For more information about this book, write:
Arkermin Project
P.O. Box 392
Medford, OR 97501

ISBN-13: 9798378637911

Ebook edition: July 2011
First mass market edition: February 2023

Printed in the United States of America
10 9 8 7 6 5 4 3 2 1

For Tom and Cathy,
taking a chance
on a boy named Charlie.

City of Thicket

c. 2011

CONTENTS

Acknowledgments

Portions of this book were revisited and updated with the advancement in technology. "City of Thicket" was originally published in July 2011, starting with the curious nature of cauliflower's central nervous system.

Mahalo to my editor, D.E. Roman, for strengthening my writing. To my significant other, and treasured forever, Elle: I couldn't have started my adventure without you. And to my children, please learn the art of storytelling so I'm not the only one hoping to change the world with the written word.

NB 157 (2218 A.D.)
Somewhere in the West Sector

Chapter 1

Celebration of Change

..

"For I consider that the sufferings of this present time
are not worth comparing with the glory that is to be
revealed to us."

Romans 8:18

..

The scalpel is extremely sharp and the slightest
movement in the wrong direction could paralyze
Shantelle's entire left arm. Without anesthesia, the pain
is on the verge of becoming unbearable. An
embarrassing tear appears in the duct of her eye. She
bites down on her lower lip, suffering through the
incision, wishing she had gone to the government
health tower to avoid this pain.

She looks down along the landscape of her arm that
lays alongside the operating table, a kitchen
countertop. The blood that quickly leaks from the
many large incisions in her wrist fills the air with the
taste of a familiar metal. She closes her eyes, trying to
block out the pressure and immense pain of having
someone dig a surgical blade into her flesh, removing
sections of skin and muscle for a benefit that slowly
slips from memory.

The tiny room is extremely bright, illuminated by
numerous archaic light fixtures that hang from cables.
A carpet of LED light bulbs is suspended across the
entire ceiling, as if the room was originally built to
gradually lighten the human race's pigmentation. An

1

inconspicuous array of copper pipes lines the inside of the walls that generate an electrical hum, creating a white noise that Shantelle uses to keep her worries at bay.

Uncomfortable and capable of passing out from the pain, Shantelle mumbles to the surgeon standing next to her. The surgeon's gown is made up of white cloth matching the off-centered paleness of the walls, blending his features, almost allowing him to vanish completely into the moments of Shantelle's hysteria. His rubber gloves are dowsed in patches of splattered blood, accenting the shaky scalpel that dives back and forth against Shantelle's wrist.

Shantelle has to keep reminding herself why this is for her benefit. She must look at the surgeon through faint, watery eyes and trust his skill with connecting her consciousness to such a small device. She tries to think of something else to block out the pain. She remembers her mother, the way she held on to her hand and the feeling of having someone who can make everything better again. A kiss on a scrapped knee, a palm on a troubled shoulder, and a gentle hug to melt the hard times is all Shantelle wishes to endure.

She must realize that once this procedure is over, she will be able to connect to the rest of the city. Soon, she will be able to blend in. Soon, like her friends, she will be able to pay for meals, record her dreams, make cellular calls, and monitor her health with less than a touch of a button. She will be able to use the new device in her wrist as a multimedia platform to enjoy, or at least digitally preserve, the last of her teenage years for others to remember her.

Shantelle has to remember the positive outcome of such a risky operation. She cannot compare it to another tattoo without thinking she could possibly die from this operation alone. She could have invested the time and credit to get her implant professionally installed, taking the chance of being caught and thrown in with the rest to be exiled. Instead, she has chosen to have her comp-uzync installed in an unlicensed medical apartment by a man who has more scars on his arm than Shantelle would like to see.

The surgeon ties off the last stitch and Shantelle jerks her shoulder back in pain. The skin surrounding the dark metal in her wrist is bright red, agitated by the stale apartment air. Shantelle straightens her back and tries to look around the quiet room, pulling her implanted arm into her stomach. Unable to ignore the splintered end of each stitch, she pinches her skin.

"Brave as you may be, you shouldn't be touching that," the surgeon glances up while organizing his tools.

"You can't tell me what to do," she continues to squeeze the neighboring skin.

The surgeon grabs her dirty hand before it contaminates the exposed incision.

"That's a really bad idea," chuckling as he holds her wrist. "Even for you."

Shantelle pulls her hand free and stares at the surgeon with a desire to slap his face. She watches him remove his bloody gloves and drop them into a waste receptacle. He reaches for a roll of white cloth and wraps her wound several times, hoping the pressure will start the healing process. He pulls out an electronic tablet from a nearby bin of gadgets and smudges his thumb into the glass surface.

"Okay, since I gave you that shot of HDCV, you gotta wait 48 hours."

"Is that what my chart says?" Shantelle leans forward, trying to see the illuminated screen that he seems to be paraphrasing.

"No, it's science --" He flicks his finger across the screen several times without looking up. "-- and you need an update."

"What update?" Shantelle repeats the surgeon's outspoken checklist.

"No --" he looks up correcting himself with a quick shake of his head. "-- wait. Imprint."

Shantelle stares blankly at the surgeon, unable to identify any accountability.

"I need the Imprint Drive to finish up."

"My unit's not ready?"

"Yes and no," he smiles, hoping to save his reputation. "Ready blank units aren't easy to find."

"Was this --" Shantelle straightens up, pulling her injured wrist into her lap. "-- harvested?"

"Well, yeah." He tries to make a joke out of the moment but is silenced by Shantelle's look of anguish. "Look, there's no damage. It's like new. The ligaments just need time to anchor. Maybe another software update. Maybe another patch. I definitely need to tweak my rooter whenever I get the time --" He trails off in volume as he criticizes his own work.

"Hello?"

"Yeah --" his attention returns to the tablet screen. "-- your device needs to be rooted and --" he pauses, looking up at his patient, "-- I still need that Imprint Drive."

"I heard you," Shantelle snaps, cradling her swollen wrist. "I'm not doing this again."

"That's okay," he acknowledges the implant with his free hand, confident in his honest answer. "You got a classic model."

"You're cheap. You know that?"

Bordering the urge to scream and cry, the pain in Shantelle's left wrist is becoming more than she can withstand. She wonders what sort of mess she has brought upon herself. She thinks back to her group of rebellious friends who encouraged her to get this implant. They assured her that this surgeon was the best in the underground market. They told her that once she became connected like everyone else, she would feel closer to her creator.

Shantelle tries to justify the throbbing pain with the circumstances surrounding the outcome of the procedure, focusing on her friends and everyone's attempt to get back into the city. She feels as if she has no one left to trust.

"Just clean me up and let me go." Shantelle holds her wrist up with determination in her eyes.

"If I remember correctly," he turns away from her, setting the tablet on a nearby table and heading toward a large machine. "I have her right here. Fresh out the box."

The surgeon drags a metal piped contraption on wheels across the kitchen floor. The dull shine in the metal surface does little to reassure Shantelle of its recent maintenance check or its own cleaning. Hanging from a canopy of wired mesh are two mechanical articulated joints that look to devour human arms, with the intent of rooting the comp-uzync system. The mechanical arms lead into a large liquid filter, and separation chamber, both of which are connected to a computer station.

"I thought you were joking."

"Oh, science is never a joke. It can tease and force its way into your head, but in the end, it's all about the bottom line." The surgeon grabs one of the mechanical arms from its home on the vine. "It's not like you have another way."

"With that?" Shantelle looks at the articulated joint, raising her brow and voice to carry her shock.

"Of course." He looks up at the nest. "You got something else?"

"I'm going to pass."

"Pass?" The surgeon laughs as he steps back and hangs the mechanical arm on the vine. "Skip step one and go directly to step two and three?"

"Yeah."

The surgeon slowly approaches his patient, tracing her tiny figure with his eyes. He places both hands on the edge of the kitchen counter, pressing his thumb knuckles into her thighs.

"I bet you do," he says leaning in close to breathe in her scent. He smiles, revealing for a single moment, a glint of insanity in his eyes.

She remains silent and looks away.

He exhales sharply, acknowledging her lack of a response.

"Pity." He walks away and grabs another tablet from a different crate of electronic devices. "Make sure you get an ID."

"Can't I get one from you?"

"Do I look like citizen registration?" He lifts the tablet and his hand, holding up her rhetorical question like a banner of stupidity, "Right this way, runaway!" He returns to his tablet, ignoring her question. "Just turn yourself in. They'll hook you up."

"You think you're funny," her tone stops short.

"Not really," he pushes his glasses higher on the bridge of his nose, looking at the dirty nature of her clothes. "Neither is my reputation."

"What reputation? You butchered my arm! You told me you had experience in this type of thing. I trusted you!" Shantelle hops down from the kitchen table and shuffles her footsteps forward. "You told me it would be ready to go and now I have to get it fixed because you can't finish? What kind of doctor are you?!"

"Hey, I never said I was a doctor." He holds up the tablet as a gesture to appear less threatening. "I just use the guy's name."

Shantelle grabs his coat, twisting the fabric around his neck.

"Okay," he starts as if conceding to the confrontation. "Fine. No charge. Keep your credits."

"I should keep a piece of you," she tightens her grip.

"You won't get past SCS."

"Not with you," she pushes him away, looking around the room for a way to insult him. "-- crutch."

Shantelle shuffles past the surgeon's chair, kicking one of its wooden legs. He looks down, turning up to witness Shantelle headed for the door. His impulse should be to confront her and demand she pay for the job he performed. Turn her into the authorities for seeking him out and asking for an illegal installation of a device given to only those born within city limits. He should stop her before she runs off, perhaps warn her of the dangers behind an infected wound, susceptible to airborne disease and bacteria.

Rather than disclose himself to Silver Collar Society, he watches Shantelle pull a lever near the door, accessing the internal mechanism of the apartment's entry-port. The twisting gears grind against a metallic surface and the harmonious chirps of a locking code resonate from inside the walls. The circular door opens by unraveling at the center, pulling apart like a starburst of cement and reseeded steel.

Shantelle steps outside of the surgeon's room, which is in the guise of a residential flat, adjacent to several

8

other apartments of Thicket's legal citizens. The décor of the floor's hallway is doused in a dreary color of beaten down brown. The ceiling is lined with thick silver pipes which run in the same direction, branching off into a compartment above each entry-port, exchanging heat, water, and oxygen.

Shantelle staggers down the hallway, holding her operated wrist close to her stomach. Her healing pains are stronger now that her rapid heartbeat is no longer distracting her from the throbbing of an open wound. With her free hand, she reaches for a button on a nearby wall, calling an elevator up 16 floors. The sound of an approaching transport reminds Shantelle of the time she usually spends with her friends. Their shenanigans would always upset the registered adults around her, sickening them to the point of ignoring her, forcing Shantelle and several thousands more like her to fend for themselves against those who would take advantage.

Shantelle remembers an episode which included her best friend, Thumbs, and the two sisters who went everywhere together. Everyone was on board an elevator headed toward the penthouse floor of an upper elite district. Thumb's plan was to follow an unsuspecting woman in the same elevator and fake the idea of being separated from their parents. As soon as she let them into her apartment, the thievery would begin. Shantelle and her friends saw no boundaries when it came to survival. They figured, if the city was to consider them as outcasts of society, scavengers of the outer wastelands, and even residents to the post-modern decay, their compensation came in the form of

9

fraud and intimidation.

When Shantelle steps into the open transport to take her down to the surface level, an eerie feeling stretches across her shoulder blades. She thinks about her father and what he could be doing at this very second. She thinks about the years she slaved to make sure she could survive without other people needing validation for her existence.

The monitors on the walls of the elevator splash the words WELCOME and PLEASE MOVE TO THE CENTER OF THE TRANSPORT, mimicking the demands of a voice Shantelle has always considered more robotic than human. The elevator's gravity drops and for a second the blood dripping from her surgical wound stays in her wrist. The transport plummets to the surface level in less than 10 seconds, gliding into a cradled stop at the bottom.

The monitors splash an exit message for Shantelle to HAVE A GLORIOUS DAY, reminding her to adhere to all SCS rules and regulations, and to get her cycled comp-uzync check-up. For the first time in her life, the latter reminder pertains to her. The elevator door opens with a pressurized release. The smells of the street invade the tiny transport, clouding Shantelle's senses with the memory of rusty metal and a heated meal. She begins walking away from the elevator and the door behind her seals shut, returning to the upper levels of the building.

The city of Thicket is crowded, jammed with thousands of pedestrians who wander the streets, commuting back and forth from their homes to the workplace. Woven like a tapestry, the alleyways and suspended walkways in each sector connect different neighborhoods of cultures and religions. Marketplaces are like zip codes that meander through the city like a loose thread, stitched into the fabric of Thicket's elaborate design.

Without street signs, Shantelle must rely more on memory than her fading sense of direction. The epicenter of the city is the population's focal point that takes the form of an extravagant cathedral, shoehorned by the encroaching districts of the North Alpha and North Beta Sector. The cathedral is rumored to be constructed entirely of gold and able to block all communication from the outside world.

Against her deafening judgment, Shantelle marches on, ignoring the cathedral while hiding her wrist. The feeling of lost energy becomes apparent as she reaches the edge of the East Sector.

Most of the East Sector is dirty with unsightly steam-exhaust vents exposed on the surface of the neuro-metal pavement for pedestrians to step around. These machines are necessary for survival, supplying the people of Thicket with oxygen and heat. They accent the city's need for repair with an abundance of rust and flammable grease that collects off the vent's openings.

Shantelle hobbles past dozens of these vents on her way, each machine in the East Sector dirtier than the last. She navigates toward a northern most alleyway that is known by many as the place to be at night. The pain in her wrist keeps her eyelids fluttering as she approaches a large circular door, guarded by a muscular man who refuses to let her in. He holds out a hand, preventing Shantelle from taking another step.

"Not tonight, Hopper. Please?" Shantelle cracks her neck with a tilt of her head, positioning her wrist closer to her stomach.

"Can't let you in this time, Lips." He lowers his hand, crossing his arms and gesturing to an inconspicuous line that has formed around the corner.

"Are you serious?" She looks disparagingly at the cluster of young adults who are waiting patiently to get into the club. "I need to get inside --" she raises her arm to Hopper's face, splashing several drops of blood against his clean, white shirt. "-- right now!"

The brutish man of a bouncer lets his shoulders fall back, rolling his eyes into the back of his head and letting out a huff of acceptance. He reaches behind him and pulls a long lever built into the door frame. The pressurized seal of the entry-port releases a gust of steam, twisting and turning gears from the inside of the structure.

"You owe me a shirt," he remarks.
"I'll get you two."

Music from inside the venue pours into the street, giving those waiting outside a glimpse into the excitement that awaits. One girl, patiently standing with a group of men who look to be her personal bodyguards, turns to the man beside her and compliments the style of music. Most expect that once inside the ESC experience, life will get easier, but Shantelle knows better.

The entrance to the East Sector Club is encased in darkness. Strobe lights of cycled colors bombard mirrored walls as patterns are traced across the ceiling. The flicker of light from a salvaged disco ball catches everyone dancing.

Shantelle makes her way through the crowd, keeping her wrist elevated and protected from those with a violent dance routine. Lining the club's dance floor are bustling tables, hovering above machines that suspend their flat surfaces with a series of magnets. Around one table a tall blonde girl is showing off her newest fashion accessory.

"Did it hurt?" A shorter girl leans across the floating table to see the silver implant.

"Not really." She tucks her hair behind her ears, revealing two small silver plates embedded in her temples. "It was kinda quick." She glances toward a mirror, catching her admirable reflection.

"I'm so jealous." She twists in her seat, unable to contain her desire to be like everyone else.

"Shantelle!" The young man opens his arms as Shantelle approaches the table, hoping to get a long-awaited hug. "Where have you been?"

"Take a wild guess." Not appeased with the way her day is going, Shantelle slumps past Thumbs and his open arms to an empty seat near the other people at the table.

"Okay -- okay." He lowers his arms and returns to his seat, raising his eyebrows at the two girls who look speechless.

"Did you get it done?" Anneli, a brunette who looks identical to the blonde sitting beside her, leans in on the table, directing her question to Shantelle who has her eyes closed.

"You mean, did I get it over with?" Shantelle holds up her bloody wrist. "Yeah, and he did such a good job that I thought I'd go back and get my chest modified."

Anneli cringes at the sight of Shantelle's wrist. She adjusts her posture, smoothing out the fabric of her black vest. Her outfit, consisting of white netting across her chest, implies she is at the age when her sense of style is more important than what people think. Her arms are covered in garments of sheer black cloth, tightened above her comp-uzync. Dark brown and red bangs cover her eyebrows, framing her long face with the intense matching color of her cosmetics. Her lower lip is pierced with a single metal pearl, glistening in the dance club's colored lights. With newly implanted dermal plates, Anneli blends in with the rest of society.

Thumbs raises a hand to his chin, scratching the stubble that will soon become a beard.

"I get it, Shen," Thumbs moves closer to Shantelle, swinging his chair in her direction and placing his hand gently on her left shoulder. "You can't hold it against him for trying." He lightly squeezes her shoulder.

"Damn -- Ease off!" Shantelle pulls away, rubbing the tendons in her collar. "I should blame you for trying. At least he did something."

Shantelle looks down at her swollen wrist and the bandage that is soaked in blood. She lays her arm on the table, allowing the weight of her appendage to be carried by the floating structure. Laci, the blonde and younger of the two girls, leans across the table with an open mouth, gawking at the intensity of the wound.

"At least he did something," he mocks with a mimic. "I didn't force you." Leaning back in his chair, he starts defending himself. "I told you -- You needed to get it done. I pointed you in one direction. What's the matter? What? Can't come up with your own plan?"

"Damn, Thumbs." Laci sinks back into her seat. "Why'd you have to go there?"

"Somebody needs to take a look at that," Anneli stares intently at the wrapped wrist.

"I'm sorry, okay?" Thumbs throws up his hands like he wants no part in the conversation. "He should have done a better job!"

"Will he take you back?" Laci suggests with an innocent smile.

"I won't go back." Shantelle looks off in the distance, depressed by her own answer. "I got to get it rooted." Her words start to slur.

"That's ridiculous!" Thumbs interrupts. "What did you pay him for?"

"He didn't charge me." Shantelle looks across the table at the two girls who sit close enough to be twins conjoined at the hip, and then back again at Thumbs. "You didn't tell me I needed an Imprint Drive."

"I thought you knew," Thumbs smiles.

Anneli and Laci share a troubled look.

"Okay, this is what we'll do." Thumbs scratches his chin, thinking of a plan to settle the disagreement. "I know a guy in Wessex who owes me a favor. He built his rooter out of-"

"I'm not going with any more of your ideas!" Shantelle looks up from her wrist and the white bandage that is now bright red, barking at Thumbs and his opinion. "I'm going my own way! I'll find a way to root it myself!"

"Yeah, sure." Thumbs laughs under his breath. "You can't do anything without me. Where are you going to find someone to root your illegal implant? You can't even convince the one you had to complete the job. What makes you think you can find anyone?"

"Because!" Shantelle stands from her seat abruptly, slightly wobbling from the lack of blood. "I know who to trust!" She departs from the table and wanders into the crowd, pushing against thrown up elbows and tossed hair.

"Whatever." Thumbs leans back in his chair, stretching his arms around Laci and her older sister who is not happy with the way Shantelle is leaving on her own.

"You're an asshole, Thumbs." Anneli moves out from under his arm and follows Shantelle onto the dance floor.

The club is packed full of teenagers who are dripping in sweat and fed up with authority. Their raging hormones keep them dancing into the early hours of the morning. The more they all dance, the more popular the East Sector Club becomes. Halfway across the dance floor, Anneli reaches Shantelle who is moving slowly through the rhythmic mob. She places her hand on Shantelle's shoulder, directing her to turn around.

"Shen," she tries to speak up over the loud music. "Don't listen to Thumbs. He doesn't want anyone to be successful. If he can't have it his way, he won't let anyone else find a way. It's just who he is now."

"I don't care about him, Neli." Shantelle holds her bloody wrist close to her stomach. "He could wander outside on his own and it wouldn't make me want to help."

"I know how you feel." Anneli looks back at the table and her younger sister who is tightly snuggled into her boyfriend's chest. "I can't get Laci away from him."

"Doesn't she see through his games? I would think your sister's smarter than that." Shantelle tries to stand on the tips of her toes to get a better view of the overly attached couple but shuffles her steps forward and back into place.

"She's smart, but --" Anneli looks away from the spectacle, focusing on a couple dancing close to her who are just as intimate as her sister in the corner of the club, and then watching Shantelle's balance.

"But what?"

"She doesn't know what she wants." Anneli steps closer to Shantelle, bridging the space. "She's too young. I don't think she's doing the right thing."

"You're five minutes older than her!" Shantelle cannot help but mock Laci's older sibling. "Don't act like her mother and tell her what she can and can't do!

You're starting to sound like him."

Shantelle leaves Anneli and makes her way through the dancing crowd. With each step, the room continues to spin but for the wrong reasons. The bright lights begin to cross in fading colors, blending together in a blinding reaction to Shantelle's loss of blood. She reaches out and grabs the shoulder of the nearest dancer, leaning on a tall, slender boy with long black hair. Anneli rushes up to catch the other arm of Shantelle's collapsing figure.

"You're in no shape to do anything on your own." Anneli adjusts Shantelle's arm to carry her weight. "And I don't care if you say no. You need help. I don't care what Thumbs says, or even my sister for that matter," Anneli takes a step toward the club's exit with Shantelle's arm over her shoulder. "I'll take care of you."

"The lights are hurting my eyes!" Shantelle uses her hand to block the strobe of colors in the dance club.

"I'm taking you to someone who can help."

"My head hurts --" She can barely let the word escape her lips.

"I know a rooter."

"No -- I'm not going back to --" Shantelle tries to form a complete sentence but can hardly find the energy to lift her head.

"Don't worry. Thumbs doesn't know about this one. It's about finding the people who can point you in the right direction. Thumbs has been giving you advice for as long as you've known him. I think it's time for a change." Anneli carries Shantelle to the front exit where the circular entry-port opens with the pull of a long handle. "You have to trust me."

"I trust you --" Shantelle can barely keep her eyes open.

"Thanks." Anneli smiles, accepting Shantelle's compliment. "It may not look like it, but I don't have all the answers. Sometimes, I have to look up for guidance."

Anneli passes Hopper at the entry-port who sees Shantelle's limp condition and uncrosses his arms. Anneli shakes her head, redirecting him from helping.

"What are you --" Shantelle looks back at the outside of the East Sector Club while focusing her walking strength on the steps Anneli supports with a shoulder.

"A little bit of hope. A little bit of salvation."

Anneli spots the crowded marketplace ahead, picking up speed as she carries her weak friend through the streets of vendors opening shop. She knows that if they slow down or stop to catch a breath, they could be caught up in an unnecessary sale. She recognizes salespeople who offer the same merchandise but at different prices. The longer they walk through the marketplace, the higher the prices climb and the harder the vendors push their products on unsuspecting customers.

"Salvation -- I don't know -- I want --" Shantelle pauses. "Something --" Shantelle pauses again, rapidly blinking and taking a deep breath.

"Are you okay?"

Shantelle steps forward from Anneli's support and huddles toward an exhaust vent that drains into a grate in the street. In a series of bursts, Shantelle vomits, expelling the contents of her stomach into the drain. With each pause, she gasps for air, crying into her hair that has fallen around her face.

The loss of blood from Shantelle's wrist continues to hinder her health, causing her headaches, blurred vision, and now an upset stomach. Anneli rushes to her side, grabbing Shantelle's hair and tucking the dirty orange strands behind her ears, wiping the sweat that is accumulating on Shantelle's forehead.

"Shen," Anneli tries to find her eyes in the web of dangling hair. "You don't look good. We need to get you inside."

Anneli looks around at the people who stare at the two young girls who are huddled in the corner. She sees the expression of disgust plastered on their faces, wondering if the hypocrites in them are oblivious to the mirrors they take for granted. In the distance, Anneli recognizes the tall steeple of the city cathedral. She then focuses back on Shantelle, positioning her bleeding arm over her shoulder to support her weight again.

"We're not too far. You can make it." She shifts her hip to strengthen her back.
"No -- can't -- go -- home --" Shantelle mumbles into Anneli's neck.
"You won't be alone, Shen. I'll make sure of it."

Anneli walks past the crowds who are gathered around the steps of the cathedral, past people of different ages and religions chattering on different levels of the elaborate staircase. She shifts the weight of Shantelle's limp body a second time, making it easier to ascend the steps without making it more difficult for the one who is not capable of walking on her own.

At the top of the steps, a young man dressed in a black robe and a Silver Collar around his neck calmly welcomes Anneli and Shantelle inside. Suddenly, he is witness to the blood soaked in Shantelle's bandages and alters his movements with a sense of urgency, rushing to help Anneli carry her the rest of the way. Anneli takes a step back and watches the young priest take control of Shantelle's journey through the 14-foot entry-port.

"Neli!" Shantelle notices that she is no longer being carried by her friend but by a stranger in black attire. "Don't leave me!"

"I'm not leaving you, Shen." She watches as Shantelle is easily supported by the strong arms of the young priest, leading her deeper into the cathedral. "I've gone as far as I can."

"What's going on!"

"You'll be fine!" Anneli raises a hand to wave at Shantelle. "They'll clean you up. Just don't fight them. Believe them. Find me when you wake up."

"Neli?" Shantelle looks back with nervous tears in her eyes, ignoring the attractive priest who is smiling optimistically at her situation. "Don't leave me!" She starts to cry into her words. "Please!"

"Remember me." Anneli keeps her hand up for Shantelle to see.

"Don't leave me!"

With Shantelle safely past the cathedral's threshold, six reseeded steel blades emerge from the floor and fan the 14-foot entry-port in a circular pattern. Shantelle's words are cut off by the sound of a mechanical turbine tearing through the air between them.

Chapter 2

Stones of Kenya

..

"Just as Sodom and Gomorrah and the surrounding
cities, which likewise indulged in sexual immorality
and pursued unnatural desire, serve as an example by
undergoing a punishment of eternal fire."

Jude 1:7

..

A hundred forty miles from the city of Thicket,
lightning clashes with the desert floor. A red hue
illuminates the night sky, casting a devilish shadow
behind the ruins of Sacramento, California. Even after
three centuries of devastating floods, destructive forest
fires, shattering earthquakes, and the rising of the
Pacific coastline, this center of the commercial district
remains a home to the last of the 1848 Gold Rush.

Spanning the rough terrain of a scorched earth, the
midnight storm blankets the only known passage
between Thicket and its anchor. Rain containing a
corrosive, falls in sheets over the land, erasing the
footprints recently set by an elder capered in black.
With each heavy step, he retraces the journey that
saved his life. His silhouette cuts through the lunar fog,
bringing to motion the only living creature on the dead
west coast.

Girdling the shores of Lake Tahoe, are the petrified
figures of vultures, ravens, and bats. Once irritated
long ago by the moon's reflection in the strong Alkali
waters, these creatures now highlight the fate of

humanity. With each burst of lightning, these stones of Kenya gleam like the immortal gargoyles of the ancient world, laying witness to the destruction of Thicket's future.

The stain of burning sulfur remains in the topsoil. Like the pillared ruins of a biblical stronghold, the rubble identified as old Sacramento illustrates the severity of neglect. Sandstorms wash in from the east while acidic rains tilt in from the west. The cloaked shadow braves the storm like a casual stroll, fearing nothing of the weather's arsenal. To many, he is thought to no longer exist. To a select few, he is called the life-giving Father.

Chapter 3

Gradient Shades

..

"He will glorify me, for he will take what is mine and declare it to you."

John 16:14

..

In the middle of the city, Shantelle abruptly wakes in the back pew of the great cathedral. Anneli is nowhere to be found, having left Shantelle to recover in a building she is told to be her shelter, her refuge, and to those like Anneli's naive sister, a home close to the end of all things.

Shantelle's arm still throbs with the pain from the prior day's botched surgery. She looks around the crowded cathedral, rubbing her left wrist. Looking down she notices the bandage is no longer soaked in red, but bright white and freshly wrapped. Her chin perks up as she hears words spoken not from the hundreds sitting quietly in every pew before her, but from the solitary man singing from the balcony above.

"Through-ough him. With-ith him. Ih-in him. With the unity-of-the-Ho-oly Spir-hirit. All glory-and-honor-is-yours, Almigh-high-ty fah-ather. For-ever and Eh-hever."

The occupants of the cathedral seem to harmonize a response, collectively acknowledging the priest. Shantelle watches people on her left fall to their knees, clasping their hands in prayer while people on her right remain standing with arms outstretched in praise.

"Take your day in strength." The priest above holds out his hands.

"Have a glorious day!" The people reply.

Those around Shantelle begin to vacate the pews. By clusters of devote patrons, the people exit through the open entry-port, leaving behind a silence that Shantelle finds unsettling. She watches the priest abandon his balcony, dragging the train of his black robe down the staircase. He acknowledges her remaining presence, and as he approaches, Shantelle shifts in her seat.

"My child," the tall, elderly man, wearing a Silver Collar, speaks in a raspy voice. "I'm glad you're still here."

Shantelle looks up at the balcony, hoping to make sense of his immediate presence. Assuming a godly demeanor, she may prefer him at a safe distance. The balcony is assembled with pillar pieces of reseeded steel, arranged in a haphazard pattern that resembles the living vine. Her hands start shaking as her attention is drawn to the reassembled glass murals that showcase the cathedral's exterior light.

"All God's children are welcome, and so stay when all others leave." He raises an eyebrow, cupping his hands together as his tired eyes trace the length of her posture to the sight of her wrapped bandage. "How's the wrist?"

"I --" Shantelle stops and turns, showing interest in

leaving with the rest of the herd.

"Harvesting is a serious crime."

"I didn't --" Shantelle's voice cracks as she begins to deflect, thinking back on her unprofessional operation.

"Expect us to look the other way?" He turns and begins walking away.

"This wasn't my choice." She reaches out to grab the priest's robe.

"Or your implant." He removes her hand from his robe.

"I didn't know!" Shantelle raises her voice, showing her distaste in their conversation.

The priest starts to chuckle. Soon the chuckle intensifies like he is thoroughly amused by the thought of an ignorant teenager. The stern echo in cathedral shows a concern for Shantelle's plight. He raises a bushy eyebrow, and a smile slowly appears. His weakened lips curl into an intimidating smirk while his many wrinkles gather across his forehead.

The priest's Silver Collar and thousands like it can be found in almost every corner of the city. Trusted as an accessory of authority, the Collar identifies those of extreme importance. Awarded to those citizens of Thicket who have shown SCS the skills and mentality of a better tomorrow, the Silver Collar for each position refracts light on a different spectrum.

For Miko, his Collar represents priesthood and communal hope, refracting a slight green tint in the sunlight. To Shantelle, the Collar symbolizes a staple of political insurgence, no matter the color on the spectrum. For Shantelle and the thousands living outside, a Collar is just another Collar when they all come out at night.

"Is that why you're here?" Miko shakes his head as he turns toward two humanoid statues, one male and the other female, near the entry-port. "Feeling safe can do something," he mumbles.

"It needs to be rooted." Shantelle whispers as she glances up at the reassembled glass. "I'm going to have nightmares about that machine."

"Beyond these walls," he turns with open arms and a stern look of judgment. "People get caught."

Shantelle's shoulders fall forward as if defeated by Miko's simple analogy. She stands from her seat and approaches the male statue, placing her dry hands on the cold, gray stone of the figure's big toe. The smooth surface compliments everything about the city, including the Collars that reside within its walled limits.

"So, then what's the point?" Shantelle looks up, gazing upon the statue's nudity, before staring into the stone's vacant regard. "I can't get an ID without turning myself in."

"Thinking that we're better off alone is easy. We can't rely on each other --" Miko approaches the female statue. "-- so it's easier to imagine the world worse off."

Shantelle's height is no taller than the priest's Collar. Her mud-stained garments look to fit someone of double stature, sinking in folds around her ankles. Her orange hair is pulled back in dust-filled braids with smeared marks of dried blood under her nose. Accumulated saliva rests in the corner of her mouth. She has tattooed on the side of her neck a set of bright pink lips. Both her hands are sullied and worn, with fingernail grime as evidence to cleaning out the filters in the Suite Oasis.

She glances down at Miko's hands, which are clean and inviting. She hears in his voice a glimmer of optimism as she pictures herself alone in a dark room without the means to escape. As the people of Thicket believe the Silver Collar Society to be their modern savior, Shantelle imagines them attending service seeking recognition. She thinks of her mother and how she helped others escape the clutches of SCS.

"Who do you think has your back?" Miko's voice grows perplexed.
"I didn't ask." Shantelle walks by, keeping her bandage above her pride.
"You know something I don't? Were you born before the New Beginning?"

Miko points to the cathedral's windows of reassembled glass. The postmodern murals depict earthquakes, tsunamis, and tornadoes. They illustrate stories of unsurpassed wildfires, the flooding of coastal cities, and severe desertification. His worn tone comes down on Shantelle's arrogance like a heavy mist.

"We were stretched to the verge of extinction."

Miko remembers how the survivors of the fortunate upper class and those left scattered across the world's five remaining continents came together. Official titles were replaced with unofficial duties. Leaders became followers of the convicted while the last of mankind fashioned their final city. Those who wore the Silver Collar became responsible for the city's state of morality under the standard of the Silver Collar Society, an organization designed to better the last of mankind.

"When SCS took over, the plan was about the people. They introduced this place," he gestures to the lack of people present, "hoping it would unify everyone's beliefs, ending the separation of spiritual order. They promised a new way of life. They promised a conclusion to religious conflict. With the help of the church, SCS promised to protect us." Miko softens his nature and proceeds to the front row pew.

"What do you mean, promised?" Shantelle moves after him. "SCS didn't save us. They're keeping us alive."

"To turn toward a higher order." He takes a step to the side, inviting Shantelle to sit. "God, if you remember, is the one with the plan."

Shantelle hesitates at first, watching the way his tired body succumbs to the weight of reclining. Miko's black garment sinks in folds on the pew, covering the wood grain with long fibers. Shantelle looks around the quiet amphitheater, finding no use in declining the offer to join him while thinking prayer is always involved.

"Shantelle, do you know God has a plan for you? A revised plan?" Miko stares off to the front of the church with both hands resting open in his lap.

"How do you know my name?" Shantelle frowns, thinking maybe she hesitated for a good reason.

"You may not have an Imprint Drive, but I know you," closing his eyes while sustaining his gaze forward. "Many names. Many faces. But one day, the flock will return."

"You actually believe God can help?" Shantelle breaks the calm, tightening her eyes in skepticism. "Not just watch?"

"For our sake," Miko keeps his attention but clears his throat. "He already tried."

The Silver Collar priest rolls up his right sleeve to reveal a comp-uzync surgically embedded in his wrist. The clean, thin border around his implant is a sign that his unit was installed in a legal, hygienic laboratory. Most illegal implants done in secret end up looking like Shantelle's: defective or previously owned.

Shantelle rubs the bandage covering her comp-uzync. Recognizing the same classic design in Miko's device, she tries to imagine a better life.

"The comp-uzync is a fascinating thing." Miko focuses on his arm. "They have opened the door to the lode of our existence. Thanks to SCS, we just may have found our link to God."

Shantelle sits in silence, tripping over the memory of nearly fainting in the East Sector Club while considering a priest's claim about God's new plan. He could have been babbling after a fully booked sermon, or he could have been sober. Shantelle did not want to experience the difference.

"How old are you, fifteen --" he assumes with a smile. "-- sixteen. For decades, people younger than you came here in search of God's truth. We get Mormons, Baptists, Buddhists, Pagans. We even get the occasional Hindu and Muslim, but we don't turn them away. We're all children of God."

"What if I don't believe you?"

"Has God ever steered you wrong?"

"Your God is wrong!" Shantelle stands from her seat to shout over the calm priest. "I would rather pray to that star," pointing to the light beaming through the reassembled glass, "than ask your God for advice."

"Calm down. Never say such things. God exists to those who are open." He gestures for Shantelle to return to her seat, "-- and SCS can show you how. If you would only let them."

"Let them?" Shantelle continues to stand. "How? By kneeling? Giving up my privacy? My security? People in line with SCS believe in absolutely nothing!"

Shantelle clenches her fists as she speaks what she believes to be the truth in a desolate world. Everywhere she travels in the city of Thicket, she assumes pedestrians crowd the streets, manipulated to think a certain way without recognizing a higher order of creation.

"The people still believe. They believe in God. They believe in each other. They also believe in SCS." Miko pushes a button on his comp-uzync, which illuminates the thin border cradling the implant. "-- and by way of connection, we can channel your beliefs."

32

The priest's comp-uzync flickers as he speaks, mimicking each syllable. He runs his fingers along the surface of his implant as if the gentle touch helps him recall the words that seem scripted to Shantelle.

"Think of this as an audition." He stands and ascends toward the balcony. "One step closer to meeting our God."

Miko presses a button on the large, reseeded steel altar and a compartment slides open, revealing a small black cube.

"Are you coming back?"

Shantelle tracks Miko's movement as he returns to the front row pew with the cube on his lap.

"Can you keep a secret?" he whispers.

"That's neuro-metal --" Shantelle scoots forward to see the tar-like pattern of dark neuro-metal, reaching out to make contact but being swatted away. "-- isn't it?"

"I need to be able to trust you." Miko runs two fingers along the topside of the black cube, creating a growling sort of purr for its wake sensor.

"I swear." Her eyes widen, hoping to convince him that she can keep any secret. "I live under the painted rock of the violet ultra."

"Do you know what this is?"

Shantelle thinks deeply on the sight of the comp-ucube, but her mind starts to wander. She ponders her existence and all she has learned, concluding that controlling misery is easy. She shakes her head.

"This is a gift with a fortune inside. With this, we can step away from SCS."

Shantelle has a hard time swallowing the priest's definition of a gift. She knows the comp-uzync is now a part of her, like a direct connection into the human soul, but she does not like the idea of being manipulated by an outside source. She looks over the bandage covering her own comp-uzync in comparison to Miko's whose is fully responsive. She runs her finger along the neuro-metal that feels like a second skin. She thinks about her mother, her friends in need, her own security, and the chance of seeing any of them again. She also wonders what it would be like to have a religious connection to the mass population of Thicket.

Everyone in Thicket is in search of the same afterlife, or so everyone says they are. The Silver Collar Society, in cooperation with the city's cathedral, are after the same goal, to give the people a personalized eternity. The most powerful organization on the planet offers the people of Thicket the chance to live forever in exchange for loyalty. While diet is mandated, dying body parts are replaced with indestructible limbs.

"Looks like it belongs to SCS."
"Don't be ridiculous." Miko pushes his hand through the air like he is moving the ridiculous question. "They don't know about this."

"They don't?" Shantelle covers her wrist.

"Why should they? They may have authority over what happens in the city, but not in here. They can't hear us in here. They can't interfere in my sermon for fear of their science being diluted." His comp-uzync illuminates, phases between several colors and fades.

"Think of the collected dreams of Thicket. Think of the fortune that lies within this device. Synchronized faith. Would you rather be on a different wavelength?"

Shantelle's gaze sinks with the feeling of shame, discovering herself as an outcast.

"Like being led away. To find the strength to --"

Miko extends a thin, translucent nanotube from the cube's corner coating.

"-- to stand up for myself."

Miko motions for Shantelle to show her comp-uzync. She begins by removing the edge of her bandage, pulling on a loose end that seems to be sticking to the rest of the dressing. With parts of her comp-uzync exposed, Shantelle can feel the cool air against the device that feels more like an irritated sunburn. She moves her left arm close to the cube, and her comp-uzync starts to glow. He offers to Shantelle the loose end of the carbon nanotube.

"Your DNA, if you please." His eyes dash between Shantelle and the tube derived from synthetic aerogel.
"Please what?"
"For your safety. I'm told it only works with organic

material." Miko sticks out his tongue and licks his forefinger, which Shantelle mirrors with the nanotube and a frown of distaste.

The priest's Silver Collar glistens with a blue-green sunlit glow. He takes the nanotube from Shantelle's hand and threads it into an access port in her comp-uzync. The comp-ucube purrs, and then growls. Shantelle can barely tell the difference.

"I'm actually quite pleased to see another Model G." Miko sits back with the cube on his lap while identifying Shantelle's implant. "The rooting process takes a few minutes. It'll clean your device and if you're lucky, unlock the secrets of the universe."

The carbon nanotube slowly illuminates and floats upward, turning into a kaleidoscope of colors. The faster the colors bleed, the darker the day becomes. To Shantelle, the room sinks into shadows of an abyss. Her eyes become heavy. She hears the purring comp-ucube, growling as part of its design, and then nothing.

Chapter 4

Everyone Needs a Pet

..

"Let no one say when he is tempted, I am being
tempted by God, for God cannot be tempted with evil,
and he himself tempts no one."

James 1:13

..

My name is Oscar Sunder. I reside in the year 2218,
one hundred fifty-seven years after the New
Beginning. As a citizen of a post-modern society
evolved from narcissistic thieves and anarchistic
leaders who paid to survive the end of the world, I
watch civilization germinate into a streaming catalog
of digital hermits. My ancestors feared a respiratory
virus that took the lives of half the global population,
but their clearly defined days of regret were well
before my date of birth, leaving me with a world that
has been given a clean slate.

Humanity was swept away in vast stretches with
natural disasters and international wars sparking
religious greed. A single empire emerged as a treaty
amid residual countries, working to better the rise of
mankind's flock. Linking those survivors, including
my ancestral best, the policy to prevent corruption
became part of Thicket's ideal. Those humbled by
recognition were given this city.

Everything in the city of Thicket is recycled,
reconstructed, reseeded, reassembled, recoiled, and
conceals an electromagnetic pulse. The streets are

crammed in narrow rows and industrial avenues, making pedestrians the main attraction. Motorized vehicles exist outside Thicket, decayed like other artifacts of the twenty-first century.

Between each of the city's many soaring circular buildings of reassembled glass and reseeded steel, nameless alleyways house the smell of homeless vendors trying to sleep under florescent showgirl signs. Circulating link-rails, seen as horizontal chutes piercing each building, commute thousands of citizens each day. These suspended neon green tubes, passing through various floors and connecting each building in a never-ending frenzy of corporate congestion, are a gift from the Silver Collar Society.

Sunlight supplies the city with a large portion of power, generating an electromagnetic pulse beneath our feet, but ultimate power does not originate from the stars. The geniuses who continue to envision Thicket as it should be feel an obligation to showcase their authority in the form of geothermal power. The prize for Thicket is to forget about our troubled past, outlining places like the wasteland as a barren graveyard. Where the Silver Collar Society sees regret, I see death.

In Thicket, sex sells faster than caffeine discs. Physical entertainment of the old world survived into what has become the largest sponsored enterprise in all inhabited corners of the city. Everyone has an opinion about selling goods and services and my thoughts are no different. Loyalty to the Silver Collar Society has allowed advancements in biotechnologies, neurosurgeries, and chemo-nutrition farms, which supplement the basic need for every living person in the city of Thicket.

Silver Collar specialists are exceptionally trained to perform certain neuro-surgical operations on the subconscious, connecting human and machine with a split-ligament cellular-device. As a licensed specialist with a personal curiosity for digital memories, my reputation in the North Alpha Sector still proves profitable.

During an era of past life dreams and horrific nightmares, my memories have come to be easy to download through the link in my surgically implanted comp-uzync. Memories considered traumatic are now capable of being locked, with the convenience of being recovered if needed, while some of my most boastful conjurations have become the hottest demand in underground retail.

Society's fixation for pleasure comes in many forms. In the last 57 years, the people of Thicket have successfully grown vertical farms on the outside of several buildings in each sector. Although the basis for chemo-nutrition was perfected within a hybrid strain of the simplest plant to harvest, the people are now more than determined to reinstate a variety of old-world vegetation into their meager diets.

Among the seeds collected from a Doomsday Vault in Canada, the cauliflower plant has proved the most beneficial to all our bio-mechanical needs. Grown in several registered buildings in the West Support Sector, cauliflower had quickly become an obsession for bioengineers and neuroscientists who could manipulate the flowers' nervous system to supply the human body with all the nutrients it would need.

The neurological activity of a living cauliflower is a map with a brain-like circuit board, leading Silver Collar specialists to further develop the technology that gave us neuro-metal and personalized devices such as the comp-uzync.

When the chemo-schematics of the cauliflower's intelligence were stolen, a neuro-hacker manipulated the plant's chemical compound to heighten their cognition. Their selfish deed led to the most precarious, most rewarding chemo-nutrient that no one openly discusses. I believe the future will play to my benefit unless the residents of Thicket stop believing in artificial hope. Until then, my concept of authority intensifies with each illegal tab I deal.

Unlike the Cauliflower press, the standard form of chemo-nutrition supplied by the Silver Collar Society, the Cau-li tab is an artificial derivative of the cauliflower; an illegal substance that supplies its user with euphoric effects comparable to any prevailing stimulant without the damaging aftereffects.

"When can I get one with full control?" A lengthy, barely covered woman lays comfortably on her side, embracing a thermal blanket and a large absorbent pillow, her comp-uzync phasing between several colors in rapid, chaotic order. "It was just getting good."
"I told you. It takes months to program," my tired

eyes follow the cold floor as I reach for my shirt. "You're lucky to get an hour."

"Mmmm --" she closes her eyes, squeezing the pillow between her legs. "-- that's just what I need."

I turn around on the edge of the bed, holding my shirt in my lap. I take in the sight of her cradled form, learning that the pattern of her reasoning has saved me from both volunteering valuable information and donating my supply of signature Cauliflower tablets. The woman moans in delight, tossing her pillow to the empty side of the bed while relishing in the assumption that the next programmed C-Tab I sell her will grant her full control of her dreams for the entire night.

"I want to go again," she mumbles.

"Oh yeah?" I mumble as I put on my shirt, covering the dispersion of little red welts across my back. "I must be your favorite."

"I thought I was your favorite," she pouts, echoing my observation with a convincing performance.

My attention to detail diminishes as I stare at her naked form. I reach into my pants pocket for a cylindrical container adorned with silver and brass. She watches as I press my thumb against a metal plate on the side of the container and allow a single Cau-li tab to tumble into her open palm.

Although her happiness is not my responsibility, I feel like I could be judged for selling her an illegal substance that will curb her motivation. She swallows the tiny pill-shaped enzyme and thanks me before rolling onto her side and falling asleep.

41

I lock the cylindrical container and notice the sound of her breathing. Her pulse quickens and she starts to whine. With a head full of dreams and my own severe anxiety, I shuffle my bare feet away from the woman's bedroom. In trying to remain calm and inconspicuous, I move toward the apartment's front entry-port.

For longer than a decade, I have been without a stable income. Making up for the credit lost, I program and sell Cau-li tabs to elite members of Thicket's upper-class as well as dealers and users on the street. As I move through the hallway in a residential tower of the North Alpha Sector, I am reminded of the disbarred recognition behind my former identity.

My name remains Oscar Sunder, but I am no longer a bioengineer. No longer am I accepted as a licensed neurosurgeon or lead in dream modulation. These days, I am an insignificant part of society. Outside the system, I am trivial, as is anyone not plugged into a social network. Without an identity, I have nothing.

Having to start my life over with no credit to my name, no medical history, and no way to prove who I used to be has been difficult. I have dealt with the impulse to jump through a panel of reassembled glass to plummet toward a more empathetic resting spot on the high-traffic street. I never wanted to deal with the truth, but as I walk alone, staring at the October skyline, I notice Thicket's bleak horizon pulling away, seeming more distant than ever before.

I massage the wrinkled folds on the back of my

neck, hoping my nervous thoughts do not turn into a migraine. Inside an elevator to take me to the highest link-rail level, I think about what my life used to entail. I remember ground-breaking theories, but I can no longer provide proof to an explanation. I remember generation-changing inventions but forced to accept that any design I offered them became property of the Silver Collar Society.

As I enter a link-rail transport station, a pod passes through the tiny waiting room. I press a button for the next pick-up and wait behind a guardrail for the next pod to appear. Link-rail passengers do not have to wait long for the next pod to come whizzing by, transporting no more than twenty at a time.

Link-rail tunnels stretch for miles through the city and operate every hour of every day, commuting thousands of citizens. The neon green tubes are made of a thick glass, reassembled from hundreds of broken televisions screens and solar panel cells. The electric current that feeds each tube, similar to light running through an optic cable, controls the ever-moving pods.

Each pod is equipped with seats, ceiling handlebars, digital monitors, and windows for viewing what is left of the outside world. I remember reading about crowded subway cars from long ago each time I enter an empty pod.

Matching the speed of the rotating platform, I walk into a moving pod and a message appears on both monitors, warning me of the closing guardrail. I occupy the window on the opposite side, staring at the back of my hands as I feel propelled toward the West Sector.

The soothing vibration of electricity in the reassembled glass around me makes me feel like I am never alone. The digital monitors signal the passing of each building. The link-rail will never stop but will allow citizens to depart at each transport station by using a rotating platform. I spend my travel time casting a stare over the horizon of the wasteland, conceding to humanity's regret.

My link-rail trips can be enjoyable. Many trips are beyond crowded when I experience encountering the people of the upper-class who should really stay in their apartments. I see elderly women who are rude and unforgiving to everyone slower than themselves. I see young men who are selfish and unloving in their unsettling decision to ignore their significant partners. I feel the constant need to mind my own business, to bury my attention in the social media of popular stupidity. The visual nuisance of today's generation is those who are deranged. They would walk all over me if given the chance.

To those who know my real name and old life, I am still considered a professional troubleshooter of digital dilemmas with a habit of finding fault in every person I meet.

The people in this city all want the same thing, and we seem to walk over each other to obtain it. The Silver Collar Society wants to give us what we need but fails to deliver in giving us what we want. Hoping to achieve full control of its inhabitants, SCS wants only the best for its people. Something I used to believe.

I may want a personalized eternity like everyone else, as stated by our government's own promise, but their price is too much. People follow SCS because they believe there is no alternative.

I remember my first transport ride when I was a toddler. I held onto my father's finger as we scoured over the marvelous view of the city. Unable to identify the different buildings that passed me below, my question was simple. Where are we going? As if I was older, I wanted to ask. What are we leaving behind? I remember the way my father used to smile, not having a care in the world, soothed in the belief that a higher order in the universe had our support.

The monitor signals an upcoming destination and my eyes pop open. I shake the restless sleep from my head as the notification for the opening guard rail comes through a speaker in my comp-uzync. The momentum within my chest pushes forward as I exit onto a rotating platform.

Adjusting to the artificial light of the West Sector, I walk into a bare corridor painted in shades of brown with a soft metallic trim. Along the ceiling's edge, insulated copper pipes run parallel through each corridor, carrying fresh water and oxygen in opposite directions. My focus follows these pipes each time I return to my apartment when it comes to my attention that a young woman is asleep near my door.

The strange woman rolls onto her knees and pushes her back upward, stretching her shoulder blades. Her dirty blonde hair tousles in front of her face as she moans and grunts, tucking her arms in as if protecting herself. Familiar with this tactic, I step to the side as she slowly wakes up.

"You okay?" I find her watery eyes.

"What?" She yawns, smiling at the level of my compassion. "Again? Slow down, champion."

"Excuse me?" I smirk, unable to recall the last time I encountered a teenager with the tenure of an adult.

"You heard me," she smiles, rolling onto her back and arching her chest upward.

"Why can't girls be normal?" I shake my head as I turn away, ranting to myself. "Seriously, what good is a promise if you're crazy --" I steal a quick glance, "-- and attractive."

My basic human intuition tells me that she is an absconder, eager to steal everything I own. The way she presents her thinly covered chest suggests she is only laying at my doorstep to entice me. Hoping to ignore her points of bribery, I place my open palm on a small glass plate. The entrance to my apartment opens after recognizing my fingerprints and she hops to her feet. Reading the time on my comp-uzync, the earliest I have ever been home without someone to meet, I notice her wandering into my apartment.

"Um --" I walk after her, now feeling unsure about opening the door. "I didn't say --"

"Way too real," she touches the hardened paint

46

strokes on a large canvas, ignoring the boundaries of personal space.

"Please don't touch," I gently grab her hand and direct it away from the painting.

"You a Collar?" She frowns before holding her hip. "Maybe you're trying to get in my pants."

"Your pants are certainly on my list of things to destroy," I look down, noticing that her pants are made of a skin-tight material that can be impossible to remove. "And I'm sure you're aware of that."

"Always," she smirks, radiating her sense of accomplishment.

"But unless you can restart the planet," I pause, referring to the painting of a lush forest, "That's the last tree."

"Oh," she blinks, realizing she is no longer as important as the center of universe.

Turning away from the painting, she gazes up at the many shelves in my apartment. As she leaves me standing unaware of her intentions, she moves to a table of discarded electronics and while glancing up, pockets a small device.

In addition to many popular gadgets that are sold in the marketplace, my apartment is filled with knickknacks and furniture from the previous two centuries. Most of my possessions are considered outdated and worthless, complimenting the dark green backdrop of my home's interior. My entire apartment is fitted as a homage to the world's past where I long to be every night I come home. I have things in my collection that reflect each of the world's most powerful countries.

Before civilization came to an abrupt decline, humans produced some of the universe's most extraordinary pieces of art. From the rubble of the wasteland, I acquired a wooden cabinet that was constructed in France, a framed mountain landscape of a castle in Germany, and part of a porcelain dish set fired in China. I can also pay tribute to the fathers of music with my refurbished compact disc player.

"Your stuff's got retro credit." She looks at her reflection in a round disc of poly-carbonate plastic.

"I told you not to touch anything." My sudden approach causes her to drop the CD.

"Shh --" she watches the disc bounce and wobble on the floor. "-- it."

I pick up the compact disc and flip it, looking over my shoulder to the music player on the shelf. I carry the player to a charging dock near the window and slide the disc into the front slot. I can hear the gears inside twisting and turning the data into audible music, and after several seconds of configuration, the vocals of twentieth-century legend Bono resonate out from two small speakers. The sound is not at all clear, resembling more of an amateur recording at an extremely loud outdoor concert.

"Sounds like it should, I think." I blink in satisfaction, deciding to leave the music on.

"Is that your girlfriend?" She quickly moves across the room and picks up a portrait of a young, brown-haired woman.

"Not exactly," I grab the portrait of Sherianne and

hold it to examine. "Do you ever listen?"

"Did she break your heart?" She asks, gently trying to pull the flimsy parchment from my grasp.

"You're still touching," I frown in irritation, firmly taking the portrait back.

"With red dirt?" She watches me fold the parchment and tuck it into my pants pocket, showing interest in my talent. Displaying a wide-trusting smile that I feel I should know from somewhere, she continues. "It looks just like her."

Her smiling eyes cross as she points a double finger pistol to her temple. Her weapon discharges and she tilts her head back as she casually moves past me.

"Are you trying to be funny?" I raise an eyebrow as I hold up my hands, following her movement across my apartment, scrutinizing her next compulsive lie.

I study the physique of this young, dirty blonde-haired freak as questions begin to circulate in my head like a link-rail with too many passengers. How does she know Sherianne? Even with my fading memory of my wife's beautiful face, I can never prove the significant impact she had on my life. I cannot show anyone a picture of what she truly looks like because none exist. And yet, this girl knows my wife. Did Sherianne escape the Channel Raid all those years ago? Is my wife alive?

I try to imagine the last time I hugged my wife or the way our legs locked together as we embraced, but no actual memory of my past comes to mind. Everything I once felt no longer exists for I no longer feel the pride of being a husband. While scanning the open area of my living room, wondering why I am still alive, I try to recall the details of the Channel Raid. My thoughts become transfixed on her assumption of my drawing, when they should be peering through the window toward the horizon in hopes of finding an answer.

Yet I know I must wait. Patience is to be had. Conditioned to reminisce over the past, I try to distract myself with practical memories. Taking strength from a miniature bronze statue of Atlas bearing the celestial globe helps me remember the importance of hospitality.

"Another brain to wash, if you ask me." She lifts her chin as she inspects another area of my apartment. "Probably thinks she's someone else right now."

"Are you a schizo?" I straighten my head and step closer, feeling pure frustration. "What are you talking about?"

The rest of my apartment is arranged like a museum. Vaulted shelves are cluttered with rare books that rest spine-out among a small facility of personal effects. Having saved my old identity cards and adorable gifts from Sherianne, I can reminisce over a bouquet of wires that represents her adoration for me. I can view a holographic love letter that looks more like a distinguished award. Worthless to most, I choose to surround myself with irreplaceable memories that prove otherwise.

Although I believe that everyone needs a hero who

tries to make the world a better place, I am not in a position to lead.

"She told me about you --" she pauses, turning to hide her vile expression. "She said you were just another broken --"
"I'm not going to listen to this," I turn away, tightening my brow over her declaration.
"Broken willow."

The tempo in the music changes and when I turn back, the girl is gone.

"God, damn it," I mutter.

Returning to the counter, I toss a transaction drive into a box of random electronics and pick up an unlatched Silver Collar. Feeling its weight in my hands, I acknowledge the control it once had over me. I carry the Collar to the window where my comfortable view of the wasteland will never leave me wanting.

I am conditioned to believe there is no better place than the city of Thicket. I am told to think that nothing needs changing. The world can refurbish the old and recycle the new. We can transform trash into something that can make humans live forever. I tumble the Silver Collar in my hands, hoping to remember the pride I felt when I first became an agent of society.

The city of Thicket is not just another stronghold against the desert winds of a dead planet, but a post-Eden haven of pirated luxury. Within the city limits, Silver Collars have seniority. We have the protection that some do not desire. Without a stronghold to encase our future, this world will again fall apart. We must accept that today's youth is capable of re-imagining a brighter tomorrow while superstitious images of a potential death bombard us all.

Chapter 5

Sea of Onlookers

..

"Behold, I send my messenger, and he will prepare the way before me. And the Lord whom you seek will suddenly come to his temple; and the messenger of the covenant in whom you delight, behold, he is coming, says the Lord of hosts."

Malachi 3:1

..

Absconders are removed citizens of Thicket, and wanted outcasts are feared for their unpredictable nature, unrelenting in lack of morality. They have come to dwell in the wastelands, despising everything about the Silver Collar Society. Evicted from living inside the city, absconders will keep Silver Collars as trophies for their rebellious ways. Some who sneak into the city refuse to leave, working the streets like a scavenger.

Anyone capable of withstanding the desert winds and extreme fluctuation in temperature either works for SCS or, as an absconder, has learned from the exceptionally best. The rough sounds of Bono's classical chords linger in my now-forlorn apartment, mixing with the confusion I see through my open doorway.

What sort of reason, I wonder, would she need to lurk? Today's youth may see the Collar as a typical symbol of governmental interference, but where they see absolute control, I see corruption. I may no longer support the standard of our government's luxuries, but I am still curious by nature.

As I pull an insulated jacket from a deep wooden trunk, I think about Sherianne's whereabouts, left in the dark and away from the people she loves. With the way I remember leaving her, nothing would have prepared me for this girl's visit. How could she know my wife? Sherianne was the most important person in the world to me, and I failed in protecting her. I failed in protecting them both. The few memories I have of my daughter begin to bubble to the surface of my guilty subconscious, leading me into merely guessing how they both could have survived.

When Sherianne and I met, we thought the world owed us a favor. We thought we would be together forever. I soon realized that one's treasure will never last, and now I am living with the devastating effects of voiding my contract with SCS.

There was a time when work was too much for the stomach to withstand. I would ingest several marbles of synthetic alcohol, not bothering to think about the consequences of destroying my liver. I hoped to drown my sorrows and forget the reason why I was still alive, only to quickly return to the guilty pleasures that I have come to justify as my normal routine of staying afloat.

I look out over the cityscape and the buildings look different now. While loading the pockets of my desert suit with my Silver Collar, cylindrical container and folded parchment, the thoughts of Sherianne and our baby girl, Jessica, flutter in the back of my throat. I swallow hard as I form their names with my lips, not wanting to say anything else out loud. With the right kind of heart, I could cry. I could wish for this life to all be a dream. I could simply be waiting to wake, but instead fall back into old habits and swallow one of my signature C-Tabs.

Within minutes of dissolving, the wave of adrenaline, followed by a rise in caffeine, mixed with the hormones of several wild animals, fuels me into taking control of my perception of reality. I scan my quiet apartment and the sparkle in my collection of silver accessories catches my eye.

As I inspect my cluttered shelf of gadgets and VR headgear, the denial of my family's existence grows louder. My heartbeat quickens with the thoughts of my family in danger, like a superhero on drugs. As I switch off the music player, the fast rhythm of my heartbeat resonates in my head, pounding with both the impulse of guilt thrown in like salt on a wound, and the brave role model who makes a recovery.

The air tastes different. Of all the temporary solutions Thicket should offer its citizens, the underground market still proves beneficial. One of my C-Tabs is enough to submerge me into a euphoric spell of harmony and exodus. A second tab allows a bridge to form within, uniting a parallel plane of self-explored fulfillment. My best voyage does not focus on the draining reality of the outside world. I should be allowed to curl into bed and let my mind wander. Today, however, requires a thicker level of motivation, forcing me to ingest more.

The light retraced from a nearby lamp illuminates the silver accessories on numerous cluttered shelves. I catch myself staring outside the window where the view of the morning's sunshine blends into a bleeding watercolor memory of Sherianne's face. The thoughts of a beautiful world dissolve and I catch myself staring into a mirror where the hard truth about my life becomes completely clear.

Soon, I can barely separate the mental images from those of reality as the world slowly turns into a darkened, yet erotic peril of misguided trust. I can no longer tell the difference between the ceiling and floor. I can no longer assume I have a stable future, and I can no longer behave like the selfish bachelor that I have claimed to be.

The vivid detail of each sky tearing tower comes into focus and pixels turn inside out in a vacuum of space. My cognition and peripherals pop back into existence as quickly as the secondhand on an analog clock. With no intention of going on an inward journey to my dream world, I head toward the front door,

A slideshow of scenarios featuring my family in physical danger stretches the muscles on the back of my neck. A feeling of guilt makes an appearance, knocking on the back of my subconscious, reminding me of the nights I came home after work, and did not crawl into bed with my wife. From the darkest pit of my wicked imagination and manifesting itself into a scenario that is breaking my existence, I feel a pain that might never be justified. I may never truly understand my dreams.

Feeling the effects of a systematic daze, I drag my feet through the corridor. The other apartments on my floor belong to SCS officials and engineers, mostly men who are married and happily involved in work-related activities. On my way to the elevator, my focus strays to the clear-paneled walls that display the city's landscape, jousting with the sky alongside other buildings that are just as tall.

I take the elevator to the floor below and walk to the nearest link-rail access point. Boarding a crowded pod, I stand near the exterior shield. The green tint in the window portrays the city of Thicket as the futuristic haven that many children of the 20th century dreamed to create. The electronic link-rail pod hums as it speeds on, almost as if the transport itself emits the sound of launching metal pipes out of the back exhaust.

The link-rail pod travels on as passengers board and disembark at each access point. The claustrophobia never makes me react as some do on the crest of a full moon, but certain busy days are only bearable thanks to a steady dosage of mind-altering drugs. My talent lies in programming each botanical brain with the effects my clients desire. Should my clients discover my former connection to SCS, my business ventures would be over. With a meaningless name and tarnished reputation, I have become a widowed scavenger.

As my pod travels through the Alpha Wing, I think back on the hours I spent configuring my bank account to collect enough credit to retire. Such is the grand design for everyone in the city and the universal agreement that SCS is in control. I depart the moving pod and arrive in a long, curved corridor containing hundreds of identical doors. Choosing a door at random, I place my open palm on a glass plate while using the digital number pad on my comp-uzync to manipulate the entry-port's security system.

To my surprise, I receive an error.

I try another door but receive the same haunting chime.

After a few attempts to trick the system into obeying a simple command, the sound of walking footsteps fills the hallway.

Two police agents of the Silver Collar Society, while dressed in darkened garments with silver collars around their neck are known simply as Collars, approach and flank me.

"Do you need some assistance?" One Collar speaks in a dense Hispanic accent, dubbing his voice in learned English.

"No, I'm okay." I quickly lower my hands, hiding my attempt to hack inside.

"Maybe not," he looks at the name on the door. "You don't have access to this room."

"I'm an idiot," I glance at the name of the entry-port. "I thought I was home."

With my best impression of portraying ignorance, I

shrug my shoulders and back away from the entry-port. Before being able to step away, the other Collar flanks me.

"We noticed you making your rounds." He addresses me in dialect I find less than intimidating.

"I suppose you like to watch." I smile, mocking his accent.

"You think you're funny?" He snaps back, unable to hide his lisp.

"Well, you are bothering me."

The Hispanic agent steps closer, casually pulling an oval-shaped device from his pocket. I watch him move two fingers along the length of the instrument, waking its sensor.

My pulse tightens as the oval splits, pivots on a hinge and flattens into two pieces, revealing a metallic cradle to cover one's comp-uzync. The memory of having my implant searched induces an anguish of abandoning my life.

"You know --" He rests the device against his thigh, pretending to relax. "People tell me the truth all the time."

"Am I under oath?"

"We're just talking," he smiles, slapping the device closed like a fidget toy.

"Good talk." I sneer as I step away. "I'm going now."

"We'll see you around, Sunder," the Hispanic agent calls out, hoping to stall my departure. "If you want to talk, you let me know."

"Can a guy be any more desperate?" I mutter.

On the elevator down, I remember the young girl in my apartment, touching everything that she thought was perhaps interesting enough to steal. I remember hearing the distorted lyrics from the music player and the way she rubbed her comp-uzync like a guilty vixen, running away as if she had something to do with my past.

The circular entry-port to the surface level opens with a pressurized release. The elevator becomes engulfed in an aroma of heated metal and hydro-generated moisture, perfumed in a layer of artificial flavors. I can taste the sweet and sourness of the street's air that is pumped through large vents all over the city. Although I keep an open eye on anything that could possibly track me to the streets below, I cannot help but feel as if I am being followed.

I venture out from behind the shadow of the Alpha Wing and Medical Tower through a small portion of the population in their busy schedules, where thousands commute on foot over streets made entirely of neuro-metal. Looking up at the connected towers of reseeded steel and reassembled glass can sometimes cause me to lose my balance. The tall glass display monitors overlooking every stretch of the marketplace flicker messages of control by SCS standards. Logos of contraband items cycle through a slide show of what not to do, followed by contact information for turning in a law-breaking neighbor.

Because of regulation by the Silver Collar Society,

the people of Thicket invest more in full frontal nudity than fully automatic artillery. The people believe in debauchery over decapitation, sex over death, and lewdness over being a prude. People of all races and languages live within the city limits of Thicket. With the government's promise to fulfill every citizen's basic need, the only ones left wanting are those who deal in the contraband and those who are willing to live without SCS. Sentences of death and banishment are held for crimes against the one company that put everything back together when the world fell apart.

Generations of both young and old have successfully adapted to a surreal existence within an isolated environment. I always find myself walking through leagues of people from different backgrounds whenever I pass the cathedral. A small crowd in the distance leads me on a trail of portable venues and while some scams of the marketplace are obvious, I can still be surprised. The merchandise is regulated by SCS and heavily taxed, forcing certain transactions into nearby shadows that do not involve a moral compass.

As I follow the embedded cable between the edge of the West Sector and the start of the Elementary Division, I feel reminded of a time I was looking forward to starting a family. For me to avoid this marketplace or any of its child-rearing merchandise, I hurry into a quieter neighborhood, dedicated to its elders and duly respected veterans. The streets are crammed with as many apartments as there are venues in other marketplaces.

Standing near a graffiti tag that blames SCS for all the city's problems, I catch sight of a florescent sign, inviting in patrons to question their standings. The sign offers fortune readings of frequenters for a price, owned and operated by Arlita and Chester Stine.

I approach the surface level apartment in the Triennial Division where I feel at home with whom many call a typical gypsy, a misfortune teller, an ill-tempered mystic, and an all-seeing oracle of doom. I ignore the accusations of Arlita being a lonely heretic against those involved in the Silver Collar Society as I must be the exception. The people of Thicket may despise her, but I see her in a different sort of light.

The entry-port to the mystic's apartment is open and looks welcoming as the atmosphere inside leads me to believe I have traveled back to an age that could never again exist. Beads hang from archways, parts of the floor are soft, metal ornaments in the shape of flowers hang upside down across the ceiling, and the air is coated in the fresh scent of artificial rosemary. On shelves that trace the walls sit tiny skulls of once-living creatures next to caged bulbs of Tillandsia, a soil-less air plant. I find an old woman in the far corner of her cluttered apartment, squatting on her chair, hunched over a lit glass orb.

Arlita's pose makes her appear younger than she really is. Her garments lay in folds of several dark colors that resemble autumn foliage, while her prestige of silver rings accents the very belief in her ability to foretell the future. Her bare feet look delicate and soft the closer I approach.

"If you stare too long, you could lose the last of your sight." I gesture with the hint of sarcasm for my friend to look up.

"Oh, it's you." Arlita moves her feet down and leans against the back of her chair. "Has it been a week? No." She leans forward and looks at the glowing orb.

"No, I'm about six --" I pause, thinking of yesterday's visit and questioning my sanity. "-- six days too soon."

"You okay?" She raises her eyebrows, quickly looking at the open chair across from her.

I approach the open seat and the orb darkens.

"Interesting. Yesterday, the orb brightened. What's been going on?" Arlita scratches at the orb, catching her fingernails in the groves that cover the sphere like intricate lace, and rotates the viewing angle.

"Nothing really. A couple of Collars giving me a little bit more trouble than usual," I squint at the darkened orb before me. "Should I be worried?"

"No, I see the Collars. They're wandering in another direction. Not with SCS. I see more of a S – O – S."

I look deeper into the dark cloud but can barely tell the difference between the shadows Arlita conjured and the shadows that haunt my own head. Within what I presume is morning fog, an image of a young girl comes running forward. The image appears blurry, but as the unknown character approaches, her face and hair color become clear and quickly fade out by stretching over the surface of the orb.

"And her!" I point, touching the glass, triggering a white noise.

"I can see. No touching, remember?" Arlita rubs the orb, removing my dirty fingerprint. "Her aura is bright, but she's lost. Another one of your clients?" Arlita cracks a smile.

"She mentioned my wife."

"Of course!" She tries to look surprised by sitting up, pulling her fingernails from the orb and severing the connection. "This time she's alive."

"She recognized Sherianne in a drawing." I quickly pull the folded picture out to show her. "She could have seen her."

"Of course, she could have." She settles back in her seat, aware of her preemptive response by nodding her head at me. "That's what you want to believe."

Arlita reaches into the folds of her extra-large tunic, pushing aside elaborate beads and metal ornaments, and uncovers a sealed container the size of a clenched fist. She pulls a latch on one side and an opening appears on the top. "After you left yesterday, a couple of teenagers stopped in my shop and traded for a palm reading."

She tilts the container and a dozen thumb-sized pieces of pressed cauliflower tumble into a haphazard mound on the table, causing the nearby orb to flicker.

I pick up a C-Tab to examine, twisting it between my fingers. "Paid in tabs?"

"Guess that depends," Arlita shrugs her shoulders. "I'm not on the C-list, so I don't know what they're worth."

By examining the bonded circuitry of a single tab, I can identify the active substance, usually depicted by a symbol. My symbol is that of a double triangle, one within the other, but the tab between my fingers is stamped with a symbol that resembles a droplet of water. Unrecognizable to myself, I pick up a second tab to compare and see a different symbol, a 5-point star inside a circle.

"I might actually miss the days of regulation." I return the tab to the pile, separating the mount into two. "Tabs were easy," I pick up a third C-Tab and examine it. "Now we get dozens of knock-off growers." I return the tab and pick up a fourth. "Some people need more to keep going these days. Maybe I'm getting too old," I toss the tab and rub the top of my balding head. "Maybe I discovered the side effects. How much do you want for them?"

"I won't take your credits."

"What are you talking about? They're worth your time. You have to take something."

"Sunny, that's the problem with society. Money gets in the way of everything. We don't have relationships anymore. We have transactions that benefit both parties, one way or another. Think about every person you've spoken to. Wasn't there something they wanted, or you wanted from them in exchange for something of value?"

I think about my clients and the mentally challenged men who try to earn an extra tab simply for being my friend. I think about the women who are responsible for the welts on my back, who I now see as pretending

65

to care when I charge extra to show a little emotion. I think about the Collars who only know how to do their job, but who take pleasure in seeing me rationalize the choices I make. Then I think about the young girl who merely wanted to find a way to fix her life at the expense of getting into my apartment.

"You're better than this," Arlita starts.

"I know," my hand softly drops on the table. "It's not like I have a choice."

"You always have a choice." Arlita reaches out to touch my wrist. "Suppose your wife is back in your life. What do you think she would say if she saw the way you swallow those things?"

"I'm sure she would ask me to share." I smile into the pile, thinking of the satisfaction in guessing each substance correctly.

"And what kind of example would you be showing her?"

"I don't know," I mumble as I sit up. "Maybe she would be okay with it."

"You don't get it." Arlita looks back into the darkened orb. "Sherianne would never want you to turn out this way. She would have wanted you to be the best at what you do."

The guilt begins to weigh me down like a perpetual downpour of human regret. Why do I feel like everything I am used to is now suddenly corrupted? Why do I feel like everything that I have become is no longer acceptable? I think about the life I briefly had when Sherianne was my motivation to fight. In my youth, I wanted to make the right decisions. I thought ahead for our mutual benefit. I planned for our future.

When Jessica came along, I was surprised as I could no longer support our union in public. I had to keep my life with Sherianne hidden from the world. These days, I look out for myself and now I feel guilty for the selfish life that is now apparent to me. I see the reflection of my face in the darkened orb before me and I cannot help but think about the mistakes that led me here.

"Is it too late for me? I mean, you know me, Arlita," I look up with a pathetic smirk on my face. "Is there any hope to get my life back?"

"Sunny," she starts with a look of disappointment. "Everyone deserves a second chance. Not everyone is willing to take that first step."

Arlita looks around her apartment and notices her husband standing in the archway of the adjacent room. Chester smiles at Arlita, nodding his head in a soft motion. He passes through the curtain of beads that quickly bounce against each other in a soothing sound of rubbing porcelain.

"Do you know why I help people?" Arlita takes both my hands into her palms.

"Paycheck," I try to smile.

"Faith."

"But you don't preach. You just listen," I blink. "And answer my questions."

"People know I believe in order. They know I believe in justice. But do they know I believe in loyalty?"

"No?" I squint my eyes, leaning back.

"Why do you think the priests in the cathedral only

speak one language?"

"Maybe they're lazy," I chuckle.

"Ordained by SCS to give the people what they need." She shifts in her seat, sitting up against the back of her chair. "They want us to believe there is no choice in the matter, but everyone has a choice. Do you understand?"

"Sort of, but why would SCS be against your beliefs?"

"Not just my beliefs." Arlita moves in her seat, preparing to stand. "If I told people to boycott SCS," pointing to her own humorous realization. "I would get thrown away."

"So, you camouflage the propaganda?"

"Because we have to," she moves to the back of the room toward a large bookshelf of cataloged binders, containing over 150 years of Thicket's history.

She traces a finger over several spines, retracing the decades of current events. The folds of her robe hang in low loops, revealing both forearms, free of any regulated implant.

"What would you say if I told you that SCS can't give us everything we need?"

"I'd wonder who could."

"If you had to choose, would you prefer the Lord of the old world or SCS?" She pulls a large binder from the shelf and cradles it in her arms.

"This is a trick, right?" I squint, smiling at my attempt to dodge the question.

"No tricks. It depends on what you believe," she gently places the heavy binder on the table in front of me. "History is worth believing."

The aged pages between the leather covers are weathered in a yellowish hue of inadequate protection. I open the middle of the three-ring binder to discover the inside spine is a reconstructed bible.

"Do other people know you have this?" I lift the corner of a page, aware of the emanating scent of pressed parchment paper that sets my mind at ease.

"Not barely enough," Arlita wanders into another part of her apartment where I hear the whistling of a steam vent. "I'm drinking tea, if you'd like a cup."

I nod my head, agreeing to her offer while indulging my thoughts in the preserved text before me.

The header of one entry is marked with a date, signed as an account from the year 2161.

The crowd erupts in a thunderous cheer. Men, women, and children alike throw up their hands in celebration of another year in passing, stomping their bare feet on the neuro-metal pavement. The year is 2161, one hundred years ago this month marks the completion of Thicket. The streets are crowded with onlookers, surrounding the steps of the cathedral with whispers of prophecy and revolution. A dozen priests stand in front of a massive sealed archway, encasing the cathedral's new entry-port. The priests are adorned with long black robes with the circular crest of our unified religion and Silver Collars that reflect the afternoon sun.

A large man with greasy hair and a jetted-out belly, wearing a similar Silver Collar, stands at the top of the stone steps with both hands raised to the crowd, gesturing for their silence.

"Today! We look to our own! Today! We look to the future! We look inward!" The man speaks with his arms outstretched, holding the attention of all those before him. "We have suffered so much these past hundred years. We have seen the outside world crumble by the unflinching winds."

The speaker pauses to allow the imagery in his speech to set in. "But today brings a new beginning! When nothing is certain, we promise you more!"

The crowd explodes with joyous cries, expecting the speaker to deliver his lines as performed in his commercials. The people in the upper class of society, standing rich in fashionable attire, are watching the celebration from open windows in nearby towers, while those in the lower class share in the same dreary garments of the great depression, watching the large greasy man speak on large display monitors throughout the city. Everyone gathered here recognizes this moment in memory for all that had been sacrificed over the last hundred years.

"With the worst behind us, I dedicate this new entry-port to the people of Thicket." He walks toward the center of the massive, 14-foot entry-port, blocking from view a small reseeded steel plate embedded in the structure's keystone. He places his hand on the scanner plate, and after a series of internal chimes the system recognizes him, not simply as the Director of Religious Affairs, but as someone with enough security

clearance to open the entry-port.

The large reseeded steel blades, interlocked upon each other in a circular design start to hum. The center keystone slowly submerges into the floor, followed by each extremely sharp blade.

A teenage boy with dark circles under his eyes glares at the speaker, refusing to join the applause while being at the center of the day's celebration. Joined by his father, wearing his own Silver Collar, he addresses the crowd.

"My name is Stephen Dakya. And this is my son, Loy. Eighty years ago, no one wanted to start a family. No one saw a point."

With his father distracted, Loy attempts to descend the stone steps of the cathedral. One of the priests acknowledges the young boy's lack of interest but stops his approach with a gesture to return.

"The world was never going to recover. We had to find away. Are you all ready to come inside?" Stephen throws his hands up in celebration.

The crowd cheers.

"We have the raw genetic material to survive through tomorrow. There is nothing we have not imagined. There is nothing we have not foreseen. We have survived the worst of disasters, and because of the Silver Collar Society, we can prepare for the life we were all meant to withstand. The next generation

will learn and appreciate the finer traits of a being a citizen." Stephen glances at Loy whose content expression turns into a surprise of intrigue. "We can teach today's youth to father their own futures."

The Silver Collar Society is responsible for the world-wide survivors who live within the city limits. After numerous countries fell victim to biological warfare and natural disasters, a private organization rallied the dozen remaining collective inhabitants across the globe to sponsor the construction of earth's ultimate stronghold.

Built against the sheer jagged cliffs of the Hetch Hetchy Valley near Yosemite National Park of California, the glacial valley seemed ideal to house the permanent residence of more than a hundred thousand refugees to the last of humanity.

"We can give them the tools to remake this world. They can re-compute the wasteland into a living habitat. They can redesign our system of belief so we will never again feel alone. Our children will lay down the next layer." He places his arm over Loy's shoulder.

The Director throws up his arms to the crowd and breathes in. "The brightest minds of the newest generation."

The priests look at Loy with smiles and nods as if allowing him to take his place among the adults is normal procedure. Loy directs his stare over the crowd surrounding the steps of the cathedral, who are eager to hear everything.

Society teaches children to rely on their own abilities, to support their own endeavors. Loy believes the prophecy will never be about him. He believes someone else will lead the people against the Silver Collar Society. Between Loy and his father, Loy is the first in his family to see the wrong in the city's standard of hope. He sees despair and an artificial means for surviving another day.

Hesitant and nervous, Loy starts slowly. "New life will be transformed by the error of our ways. Electronic control of the ways we relate." His eyes search for the Director who is now part of the crowd and still smiling in his decision to allow a teenager to speak. "A collection in a cube and a mass serving madness. A new age of regret with power and sadness. Collar rule will lead to ruin. Trust not few for new world destruction. Bar codes tailored to tainted souls. Absconder ordered with dismissal."

The crowd starts to whisper, hoping to confirm what many believe to be a joke.

The Director drops his smile and unfolds his arms, grinding his teeth as he speaks into his comp-uzync. Loy catches the sight of several Collars moving through the crowd toward the cathedral steps. Three Collars wearing gas masks surround him, reaching for his arms and face. Loy breaks free, dodging one grab and slipping through another. He runs toward the open archway of the cathedral.

"Arrest him!" The Director points to the

cathedral's entry-port, demanding the priests close off the only way for Loy to escape.

A young priest places his hand on the scanner plate, activating the entry-port's mechanized pulley system. In a sudden burst of elevation, the six reseeded steel blades fan upward from the floor below. Following Loy through the narrowing archway, one of the Collars stumbles onto the open track. The six blades tear through the Collar's head and pass through the right half of his torso.

Those close enough to see start screaming.

The Director stampers to the top of the cathedral steps that is covered in blood. The deceased Collar's hips and legs continue to twitch and bleed out, draining into the entry-port's blade cavern below. The Director speaks into his comp-uzync.

The video footage of the Collar's death fills every display monitor throughout the city. Citizens in their high-rise apartments can relax and watch the next installment in modern television. The people on the streets below scramble for the steps with outpourings of justice, demanding the return of the teenage boy, wondering what will become of him. Loy's father, frantic in the hysteria, is arrested by two Collars and escorted in the opposite direction.

Of those remaining, the youngest priest watches as the crowd disperses in large segments, each with its own unrelenting outcry of questions. Who is this teenager? Why is the Silver Collar Society threatened

*by his beliefs? Why would he think the people of
Thicket are in danger? Where is God in all of this?*

*To save the city from riots and an uprising of
anarchy, the digital monitors that hang over every
marketplace corner and residential avenue begin to
display censored footage of the Collar's death,
branding the teenage boy a murderer, a traitor, and a
terrorist to those around him.*

*To many in the city of Thicket, the Silver Collar
Society is their savior of the New Beginning. A private
organization branded as a type of government in
control of everything.*

"Do you believe him?" I call out my summary of
the transcription.

"He drew in a new wave of absconders." Arlita
returns to her seat with a steamy cup of tea, reaching
out to close the binder with a heavy flip of the back
cover.

"Maybe he was cut from the parade," I try to smile
at my own joke but find no amusement in my
company. "Okay, maybe he knew something about
SCS and they took care of him. Secrets are bad."

"I know you think reputation is important, Sunder."
Her old eyes gaze deeper into the darkened orb that
continues to flicker. "But some things are not worth the
pain."

"I know," my eyes shift across the room, not
wanting to feel guilty.

"How are you sleeping?" She does not look up as
she sips her tea.

Thinking back on the last couple nights, I remember wandering through the same dream. Images of a translucent nano-tube and the growling effects of a world-changing device invade my mind. I am endlessly being devoured by neuro-metal, molded into the pavement of the city streets.

"I'm seeing the cube again."

"Are you still running scared?" She looks up with a raised eyebrow.

"Sometimes." I look back and start counting the number of hanging beads. "Collars keep showing up, holding me back."

"Technically, they own everything you make," she tilts her head in sympathy.

I shrug my shoulders in agreement. I will never agree with the rules of invention, forcing citizens into creating new technology, presuming to be used in good faith, only to be altered and left with no reward of accomplishment.

"Not everything," my focus returns to the darkened orb.

Arlita approaches the back wall, layered in copper pipes. She loosens and swivels a pipe away from its connection and a hidden cavity is revealed.

"I made you a promise a long time ago." She pulls a cloth pouch from the copper pipe. "You told me to hide this and only give it back to you when things were too much for you to handle. Do you remember?"

"I --" I accept the pouch and loosen the string that

runs through its opening.

Recalling the moment I entrusted Arlita with my secrets, I empty the pouch into my hand and a small Imprint Drive tumbles out. My heart sinks and I can feel the excitement coursing through my veins, but I am unable to smile.

"I expected to at least get a smile out of you. Isn't that what you want?" Arlita returns the copper pipe to its original position and sits back down.

"I should be happy," I look up from staring at the ID.

"Are you scared of your past?" She smiles, popping her question with the smack of her lips.

"I've been without these memories for so long. I don't know if I can handle this kind of reunion."

"Nothing bad is going to happen to you, Sunny." She reaches across the table, hoping to touch my elbows.

"I want to believe you, but I'm sure this is going to get me into trouble." I squeeze the ID.

"I don't think SCS is aware of what humans are capable of. We can learn from our mistakes." She picks up her tea and swirls the cold liquid.

"But we're never forgiven. Not many in this city are normal." I watch Arlita lose interest in her drink. "The entire population is plugged in."

"More than half a century later," Arlita starts. "And they still fear that boy."

For anyone to be exiled from the city of Thicket without protection means a slow and hallucinating death. Loy Dakya, like many banished before him, was

77

absorbed into an absconder camp and able to survive without the assistance of the Silver Collar Society.

"No one lasts that long," I mutter as I stuff my Imprint Drive into one of the many pockets of my self-sustaining desert suit.

"Does the phrase, 'Broken Willow' mean anything to you?"

I tighten an eyebrow as I pull the cylindrical container from my pocket and deposit the remaining C-Tabs.

"Your confidence not only amazes me, Sunder," she slowly stands. "It frightens me."

"It's not the best thing in the world, but next to it," I laugh as I lean against the table.

"And yet the worst remains hidden." Arlita moves closer, taking my hands into her own wrinkled clutches, while looking at me with smoky gray, pupil-less eyes. "I wouldn't ignore all that has happened. Your wife is alive."

"Are you serious?" I lean away from her.

"This time, you have to trust me. You'll come back eventually."

I pull Arlita in for a friendly embrace.

"Kids these days. Same time next week?" I can feel her warmth like a grandmother who has enough love to heal the world.

"If you remember, sure." Her arms fall to her sides as our hug concludes, returning her focus to her tea and the darkened orb.

As I exit the gypsy's apartment, the orb brightens, flickering through the cracks in the reassembled glass. With the pressurized seal of Arlita's entry-port behind me, I wander back into the crowded streets of Thicket.

The people outside Arlita's apartment look older than me, filled with experience that I can only hope to obtain. With all that I have seen, the reality of Thicket is a tall-tale of disease. Without restrictions on prenatal health, unlicensed children have become common. One dirty child runs by, reminding me of the young boy who started a revolution, when prophecy was still sacred to half the population. Today, the same rumors are retold through legends of a second rebellion.

The various marketplaces of Thicket are occupied by small vendors who try to earn an extra credit from others on the same route. The neuro-metal asphalt is dressed in layers of recycled fabrics, trinkets constructed of reseeded materials, and advertised oddities performed by dramatic actors. Even the labor-friendly prostitutes on street corners in each sector have an angle to work.

The tall glass display screens above the marketplace flicker various messages and advertisements. When new patrons enter the area, tiny sensors in each screen track the visitor's movement. As I venture across the marketplace boulevard, bulletin screens recognize my comp-uzync signal and adjust their advertisements accordingly.

One appealing jingle always deserves my attention.

The video advert that accompanies the melody is boring but the narration, spoken through the speaker from my comp-uzync, is clear.

"Are you ready for death? Are you prepared for the afterlife? Tomorrow could be your special time. So, register today with After Dark and you won't have to worry when your special time comes. No medical bills. No embarrassing scene. No need to worry about benefactors. Stage your final bow and prepare with After Dark. Call today, before a special tomorrow. Aa-Aa-Af-Ter-Dar-Ar-Ar."

As I continue walking, the After Dark melody stays settled with my memory while my internal judgments bounce around like the verbal offers I receive throughout the busy marketplace. On my left, where a man is already negotiating a deal on the price for a re-manufactured hydro-generator, I think of what my wife would say.

Linking people together over a social network, the city of Thicket allows people to use the same government-issued implants to stay connected. Wearing sensors that distort reality is common for the younger generation, who prefer a virtual interface in the form of Jip visors. On my right, near a woman winking her way into the purchase of a set of synthetic gloves by revealing her bust, a teenage girl with dirty blonde hair moves past me in a hurry, brushing against my suit.

The possibility of Sherianne's existence has me trembling with the fear of the unknown. Now that I know she could be alive, what am I supposed to do? While the shade of blonde quickly pulls away, overlaying the other pedestrians, I dart for what I remember as an absconder with an ulterior motive.

I reach out for her shoulder, turning her around.

"Don't think you can --"

The girl's hair color quickly dissipates to an unnatural shade of orange and then a florescent blue. Her facial features transform, and I soon realize I am restraining someone wearing a Jip face shield.

"Let me go!" She tries to squirm free.
"What the --" I release my grip but look her over "-- Jip?"
"Are you blind?" she insults, gesturing to the embarrassment behind her.
"Whatever --" pushing her to the side. "-- brat."
"And?" She moves after me.

My annoyance turns cold as I try to ignore her, knowing that I am wrong while maintaining she could never be right. Suddenly, someone kicks me in the back of my knee. As I stumble to the ground, someone grabs my arm, dislocating my shoulder. Fearing my safety, I stay down while the girl in the Jip mask approaches.

"And what about the rules? You expect us to behave, but underneath --" she leans in close, smelling me through the Jip mask that distorts her features. "-- you don't care. You never did." She unzips my desert

81

suit and searches my pockets, finding the cylindrical container, Imprint Drive, and folded parchment.

I try to break free, watching in desperation as she runs away clutching her stolen ware, I notice her drop the parchment.

Once released, I feel like my masculinity will never recover. Retracting my injured arm, I fall to the ground.

Citizens of Thicket are aware of the rules that govern our streets, claiming that SCS oversees the disbursement of justice. While they must comply with SCS regulations, the citizens of Thicket are also conditioned to refrain from interfering in any crime, arrest, detention, punishment, or execution. No one feels threatened by SCS presence, nor do they protest justice as it is dispensed. As I look around the marketplace, I notice all the other patrons simply look the other way, leaving me feeling alone in a sea of starving entrepreneurs who know better than to cross the city's government.

"Another reason to not care," I mutter as I reach for the parchment.

I want to believe that everything is normal but gazing up at the building that blocks the sunlight from reaching the pavement, Thicket's skyline pulls away from my vision. Clashed with the constant gray of a scorched sky, the background of Thicket's sunset reminds me of the way Sherianne chose to keep her pregnancy a secret.

Chapter 6

Lips That Bite

..

"You shall not worship the Lord your God in that way, for every abominable thing that the Lord hates they have done for their gods, for they even burn their sons and their daughters in the fire to their gods."

Deuteronomy 12:31

..

Powered by the scorching sun and fueled to keep the city comfortable year-round, Thicket's design is the culmination of space habitation and planetary colonization. Though certain neighborhoods lay hidden by elongated buildings, the people of this city do not feel alone, but by maintaining an acceptable level of fear in several million residents, the Silver Collar Society is able to govern using unhinged authority.

With each step through the marketplace, remnants of my stolen memories begin to crystallize. My thoughts circle dirty stares as I look around, unable to make a connection to anyone I pass. Along the edge of the marketplace and between the dark alleys of Thicket, I hear people speaking a language I do not understand. Shadows of individuals move between side streets in my peripherals as I think about my stolen cylindrical container.

For over a decade I have accepted the reality that I am alone. By believing that Sherianne died in the Channel Raid, I lived with the guilt of being solely responsible. Without her, I lived with a secret I could not share. Like a widower unable to be consoled, I feel nothing for the outside world.

The further into the dark alleyways I wander, my mind becomes more abstruse. I drag my bare feet along the surface of the neuro-metal pavement, meandering through the North Beta Sector hoping to understand why I am not in my apartment. With the memory of a big misunderstanding, I feel blind in knowing why I am at fault.

My comp-uzync flickers and I feel a tingle. Trying to maintain my sanity, I acknowledge the system in my wrist to be chiming with an alarm. I look down and see the words INCOMING CALL plastered on the tiny screen. When I raise my comp-uzync closer, making it easier for me to read, a person walking by glances in my direction, hoping to eavesdrop on my conversation.

The caller's identification comes through as unknown, but I feel compelled to answer the incoming request. Unwilling to be seen, I speak into the microphone.

"Hello?"

There is no answer. Instead, I hear faint voices on the other end, male and female lingo with loud noise in the background. I can barely make out the conversation.

"Where'd you get this?"

The first voice sounds male and brutish, as if it

resonates from inside the body of a large block of stone.

"Why should it matter? There's nothing wrong with it."

The second voice sounds female and weak, as if it is bubbling from an innocent child with a not-so-innocent angle to work.

My comp-uzync fills with static and I hear the female start to cry.

Her soft murmurs quickly turn into a roaring laughter. The static gets louder as the sound of a pressurized seal overpowers the tiny speaker in my implant. Music fills my comp-uzync, forcing me to lower the volume. I look around, realizing that this call is coming from another part of the city. I speak into the microphone again.

"Anyone there?"

The call disconnects and my comp-uzync returns to its normal, idle state. I access the call history in my implant's mobile communication application but find no information on the call's origin. The streets are quiet again, but in the distance, I hear a vibration that many associate with music.

As I look through my comp-uzync, a group of teenagers walk past me. They are dressed in today's fashion, which I personally find inappropriate. According to society's ever-changing standard, guys will always be expected to dress for utility. The modern male is often identified by loose-fitting pants that hide the waist, while girls are expected to dress for appearance, wearing tight-fitting leggings that accentuate their physique. When they turn down an alleyway, I decide to follow, maintaining my distance.

Soon, the smells and sounds of the marketplace are far behind me. In the approaching distance, I spot a half dozen people standing in a conversation. A single brute of a man in light attire stands near a plain entry-port. As I approach, everyone turns toward me with disapproval and resentment, voicing their opinions to each other as to why I am here.

"Long night?" I rub the top of my face, looking up at the bouncer.
"Not long enough." The bouncer flexes his shoulders, cracking a bone I cannot identify.
"What's going in there?" I point to the entry-port.
"Business."
"Those kids here for a meeting?" I tilt my head back, gesturing to the group over my shoulder.
The bouncer ignores my question and uncrosses his arms, pushing me to the side to acknowledge a familiar face approaching the entry-port.

In the East Sector Club, popular for its strobe shows and arcade games, people take refuge from the streets of Thicket and the reality of SCS control. The bouncer escorts the high-ranking SCS engineer and his guests through the heavy entry-port that opens and quickly shuts. The darker stained habitat of raging hormones and illegal circuits dancing to the synthetic beats of an electronic jockey is revealed for a moment before my view is hindered.

Knowing the limits to interrogation, I back away. I wander toward a cluster of steam vents and watch from a distance, keeping an eye on those who exit the club. Trying to remember the faces of those who stole from me, I throw my head back and look up, hoping to wake from this nightmare. I close my eyes and with a state of depression turning my stomach, I sink to the ground. Wrapping my arms around my knees, I bury my face in my elbows.

A few seconds later, I look up at the club's entrance and see that the people standing nearby have been granted entry. Resting my sense of defeat, I turn my head and spot something silver in a puddle of steam exhaust. I reach for the object and discover the silver and copper design of my cylindrical container.

With a pessimistic shake, I hear the rattle of several C-Tabs stored inside. Turning somewhat optimistic about finding what was stolen, I ingest a tab and like a rush of adrenaline to start my day, the motivation to save my family brings me to my feet.

The more I think about my wife, the clearer my intentions become. I picture Sherianne holding our daughter, determined to survive against the world of SCS. Picturing her alive, I return to the entry-port.

"I'm looking for a couple of thieves."
"Yeah, I can see that," the bouncer glares down on my thin hairline.

"You like girls with green hair?"

The bouncer does not move, nor is he amused by my accusation.

"What about a dirty blonde?" I squint in his direction.

The bouncer's rigid posture breaks like chiseled ice. The muscles in his arms appear to loosen at the seams.

"There it is." I mutter, raising an eyebrow while seeming surprised I scored a direct hit.

He looks back at the heavy entry-port, almost as if hiding his flushed reaction. Turning back to me, he asks, "What's in it for me?"

"A new shirt?" I glance down at the sprinkle of blood that does not match his range of motion.

"If this was your blood, I wouldn't see a problem."

"Did you see her with anyone?" I do my best to show patience.

"Look pal, unless you plan on paying for information," he looks over my thinning hair and desert suit, swiping his nose with a massive thumb. "You don't get in."

"You let Collars in? Don't you?" I smile, stepping past the bouncer to approach the heavy entry-port.

"You don't get in." The bouncer does not seem amused, pinching my shoulder.

I maneuver away from his grip, holding up my hands as if to apologize.

"Are you trying to piss me off?" He steps toward me, forcing me away from the entry-port.

"I mean no offense," I place my hands together, wedging the air under my nose. "I just really need to get in."

"You and everyone else." He waves me away. "What makes you special?"

"Look," I lower my hands. "My name's Oscar. I know you're having a tough night. I can see it in your shoulders and they're not making it any easier. I've been there." I glance behind me, checking to see if we are alone. "Teenagers think they're entitled to everything. They're digital hipsters. They treat the world like a never-ending supply of principle payments and ignore authority like a curfew."

"What's your point?" He relaxes his shoulders, seeing me no longer as another obstacle, but as a human being.

"Adults need to stick together. I know you're looking out for me, and I appreciate that. When the time comes, I'll owe you my life."

Luck resides with my unusual habit of being entwined with other people's lives. The more I empathize with the bouncer's position of authority, the more I am reminded of the life I lost in taking a stand for love. Hoping to stay clear of any disarray, I apologize again.

With a sympathetic nod, the bouncer opens the heavy entry-port and allows me to enter the East Sector Club.

Occupying the center of the large room, teenagers

dance behind railings that cage them in. The dance floor sinks below a couple of steps as if the entire platform is a covering for something below.

The sides of the club are occupied by numerous arcade games that emit virtual controls of colored lights and three-dimensional viewing screens. Countless credits are spent by dozens of energetic patrons vigorously trying to outperform previous high scores. Taking comfort in a far corner of the club, a young man and his female companion sit at a suspended table with a waitress nearby.

"Three ND's." The young man speaks to the waitress.

"Three nicotine discs. Table nine. Eighty credits."

"Now that's a deal!" He snaps with a smile, accepting a transaction drive being handed to him by the tall waitress.

The young man inserts the transaction drive into his implant and allows the deduction to be made from his bank account. He hands the drive back to the waitress and receives three tiny discs, each as thin as aluminum foil but as dark as neuro-metal itself. He passes a soluble disc to his companion, and she inserts it into her implant. As if a wave of nicotine crashes down on her, she sinks into her chair.

"Can I hold that one?" She leans in, begging the young man for another jolt.

"She's on her way." He tries to distract her from pocketing the remaining nicotine disc by pulling out a transparent visor. "Wanna try my new Jip?"

"Yes," she sits up, unable to contain her subtlety.

The flexible material of the Jip mask is designed to display an interface worthy of the next generation. She attaches the electronic glass to the silver plates embedded in her temples. As if activated upon request, the Jip mask creates an unbelievable simulation for anyone to experience.

"See that wave in the shield?" He points to a repeating pattern in mold.
"Uh --" she looks around. "-- oh yeah," she mumbles, unwilling to remove the visor to see or return to reality.
"It blocks AI."
"No way. So --" she pauses, thinking of the rest of her body. "-- like, I'm invisible?"

Most of the people who work at the East Sector Club are easy to recognize but not easy to stop. Several waitresses scurry around the dance floor on wheeled footwear, distributing aqua-marbles and taking orders. Their black uniforms with the neon blue letters ESC give rise to the club's reputation for being the only venue in the city where one can escape.

"Excuse me," I reach out and grab the attention of a rolling waitress on her way across the room. "I'm looking for a girl with dirty blonde hair."
"Honey, you've got to paint it on thicker than that." She tries to move on. "Every man in here is looking for some girl to call him daddy."
"I think she's hiding here."
She sighs, "Did she steal your heart?" She slowly

91

pulls her florescent blue hair from the corner of her mouth.

My eyes lock on the waitress's smile. I feel lost in her beauty, like a child quickly recovered from a bad dream. I remember Sherianne and the way she smiled at me after I told her how much I loved her. Like the ripple theory in reverse, I think about the girl in my apartment who told me that my life was a lie, and that my wife is alive.

"Are you okay?" She touches my shoulder. "You look like you're going to be sick."

"Yeah," I hold my forehead, suddenly looking at the floor.

"You think you can run," she smiles, leaning in close to be heard over the music.

I back away from the rolling waitress in sheer paranoia, but she wraps her arm around my neck like we are best friends. Her perfume is intoxicating, reminding me of soft fabrics and animal urges. Close to my face are her tattooed fingers with the letters, T, R, U, and E, highlighted in black ink. On her other hand, she shares the feeling of her uncovered hip with the letters, L, O, V, and E.

"What are you doing?"

"There's no need to run."

"I'm not running." I try again to break free but feel like pudding in the arms of the blue-haired waitress.

"Right, and gold is worthless." She lifts my left hand, highlighting the gold ring around my pinkie.

I feel a loss for words, unable to think of anything but the fact that I look like an absconder living within the city, wearing everything I own. Without a way to prove my intentions, I feel reminded of the scavenger traits that match my life exactly.

"Let me hold that ring for you."

"That's not going to happen."

"Okay," she releases me, sounding unconvinced. "Good luck with that."

I hold up my hands to stop her from rolling away. I can tell by the way she bites on her lower lip that she cares more about her own luxury than the reputation of the next absconder who uses the club for personal gain.

"How much for a name?" I utter.

"Enough that you'll ask for more," she returns with a prettier smile, looking around as if her supervisor could catch her without an order to fill.

I look past her blue hair at a table of teenagers who roar in laughter, rousing a curious stimulus for everyone in the club. The suspended table that hovers before them projects a holographic recording of a young man and his two female friends. The reflection of light from a series of lenses built into the glass surface of the table flickers in a small cloud of electronic dust, illuminating the darkest corner of the East Sector Club with the illusion of live footage.

"What's with the show-all?" I nod at the table.

The waitress turns to guess and sees whom I am referring to. "Oh," leaning back to elaborate. "Young growers. A little weird if you ask me, but at least they keep their word."

I know many growers in Thicket but feel lost in my stare when she speaks of them as usual contributors to the East Sector Club. As do most people in the city, I use the term grower as being synonymous with programming a botanical enzyme, but the city's youth will continue to surprise me.

The waitress sees that I cannot help myself. She smiles to break my line-of-sight and makes an offer.

"I'll introduce you for a set of C's," she offers.
"What makes you think I'm growing?" My gaze snaps to her lips that are close enough to kiss.
"I can tell," she tucks a strand of hair behind each ear. "I may be shy, but I can tell."

I reach into the zipper folds of my desert suit, and from between layers of neuro-metal fabric I pull out the cylindrical container. I press my thumb to the metal plate and a compartment opens. I remove what the waitress assumes to be two C-Tabs before stuffing the container back into my suit.

She reaches for my closed hand.

I pull back, "What do you mean, you're shy?"
"Alright, not shy." She reaches out again but returns empty handed. "I'm hungry."
"Being hungry is worse?" I retract my closed hand to my chest. "I never thought of it that way."
"They don't know a lot of people."

In the busy darkness of the active club, I stare at the occupied table, judging the young man's appearance based on hearsay. Along with his female companions, one blonde and the other a dirty shade of orange, they look close together in age and capable of surviving on their own.

"They're the kind of people who hate authority, and don't take kindly to absconders, so I wouldn't show off any trophy you have. They deal in growing nightmare fuel and never rate my orders. Now what about our deal?" The waitress moves in close.

"What symbol do they use?" I slowly extend my closed hand.

"A little of everything." She reaches for my hand, covering my fist. "Sometimes a pentagram, sometimes an arrow. Are we settled?"

"Not quite." I turn my fist over, giving her a chance. "Do they know what you think of them?"

The waitress looks at the table of teenagers that is no longer drawing on spectators with their holographic light recording. I make my move in their direction, but the waitress digs her fingers into my cupped hand only to find it empty.

"What gives?"

"It's okay," I hold out my hand to assure her of my task as I move toward the suspended table. "I can introduce myself."

On route to the table, I hear a portion of their private conversation.

"We get what we need, we'll be in control." The young man speaks with his elbows on the table, directing his concern to the girl with blonde hair.

"If we let him do all the work, we won't need Father anymore." The other girl points out without mirroring his hunched position.

"Imagine what this place would look like --" he leans in. "-- if we had everyone in mind."

Upon approach, the table goes silent. Being the only one who could resemble authority, I take their sudden shift as my cue.

"Looking for a good time, old man?" The young man speaks, glancing sideways, expecting both his companions to laugh.

"I'm not your type," reflecting my content.

I slip my hands in my desert suit, feeling the weight of the cylindrical container. As I fidget with the silver and copper inlay, my memory stirs. I remember my visit with Arlita and reading about a young boy who started a revolution.

The young man has features that barely set him apart from the other scoundrels on the street. His dark brown hair is long and disheveled, covering part of his face like a tapestry against a civil introduction. His face looks clean and smooth, and by the way he rubs his jaw line, he cannot wait to start shaving off a beard. His mock desert suit looks cheap and faulty, making me wonder how well off his business really is.

The blonde girl whispers to the young man, darting her eyes back at me.

"I'm looking for someone." I move to take a nearby seat.

"Nobody said you could sit, old man." The young man snaps, but it is not enough to sway me from grabbing hold of the padded chair.

"He could be SCS," the girl with orange hair proudly claims.

"What if I am?" I correct her assumption. "I'm looking for a thief."

"So, what does that have to do with us?" The young man leans in, intrigued.

"Word on the link tells me that absconders grow in closed circuits." I stretch in my seat, admiring the comp-uzync implant on the young man's forearm.

"Not closed enough, apparently," he huffs.

The synthetic music from the club bounces off each mirrored wall, aiding the strobe lasers and beams of spotlights that shoot across the dance floor and break apart in the reflective surface of the disco ball. The girl with orange hair glares at me, aware that I am not about to stand and casually walk away.

"Was it Anneli?" The blonde asks but is immediately elbowed in her seat by the young man.

"Zip it, Laci."

I lean forward with tensed shoulders. "Is that her name?"

"I dunno," Laci smiles and rolls her eyes, looking away.

Laci's young demeanor seeps out in her overuse of cosmetics. Under her bright blonde mane is a crop of pitch-black hair. Through the bridge of her nose is a piece of silver that many men find attractive. Her eyebrows have been plucked and painted on with a series of piercings that line her innocent brow. Her earlobes are stretched and pierced with large gauges of neuro-metal plugs and the crescent phase of our abandoned moon is tattooed down the front of her neck. She is dressed in layers of black and white fabric, with alternating straps and belts of artificial leather. Seemingly lost in thought, she continues.

"She said someone was following her."

"My guess's locked in." The young man tilts his head at me.

"Was she selling?" I ignore his remark, looking at the young girl.

"I dunno," Laci sits back in her seat.

The young man interrupts, "Not that it concerns you."

"Are we negotiating?" I snap at him.

"As a matter of fact, we are," he leans in across the table.

"Thumbs --" Laci pushes him in the shoulder. "-- what the hell?"

"Look, old man," Thumbs starts. "Unless you pay for our time, scrutinize somewhere else."

Raising my hand, I signal the nearest waitress.

"What can I get you, sir?"

"Get me a marble of Alco. D grade." I feel willing

to settle for anything at this point.

"I'm sorry, sir. We don't serve Alco-synths."

Shocked, I nod and let the waitress roll away, deciding against any type of refreshment.

"What a dumbass! This is a dance club. What did you expect?" Thumbs laughs with a slacked jaw, throwing his head back.

"He needs a girlfriend," Laci whispers in his ear.

"Yeah," he adds, pointing me off. "Get your own, grandpa."

I rise from the seat and look out at the sea of dancing fools. Many of them are dressed in minimum attire, including varied patterns of neuro-metal cloth, and vest-like coverings, attached with refitted rubber straps. As I wander through the crowded dance floor, men sway and glisten with sweat on their bare chests as do women with their flat stomachs and hypnotic pheromones. The hotter months ahead will only shed the layers off each dancer, while the colder months mean more voltage through each able body. Mimicking fish that used to jump over riverbank crossings, everyone bounces to the steady beat of Thicket's popular culture.

On my right, I pass men with long black hair trying to break their own necks to the rhythm of the hidden speakers. On my left, I try to ignore the same "True Love" waitress who is busy flirting with another unsuspecting patron. Quickly, as if on cue with the rhythm, the music stops and the colors in the room start to bleed. The flailing limbs and kicked-up shins of nearby dancers seem to transform from the tendons and tongues of wild, ferocious creatures into rigid corpses of the ill-entertained. Everything beautiful about the East Sector Club falls apart in a moment of decay. They call this dancing apparently, and everything pure and sweet melts into a scale of sepia-toned flashes of dilated pupils and widened smiles.

Suddenly, a male dancer in the crowd howls, a female dancer screams, and the beat drops back into circulation.

I look back at the table in the far corner and notice the young man and his two female counterparts are now accompanied by a fourth. An individual in dark attire is reaching through the holographic image, distorting the video footage.

I move toward the table, eavesdropping on their conversation.

"He wasn't going to leave."
"I don't really care. We had a deal --" Thumbs pauses the hologram, sensing my presence, "Yes, Digis?" speaking through the still projection.

I hate the term, Digis, as this common insult for the older generation refers to the post digital era as archaic. Like another piece to an abstract puzzle set in motion, the accusation sparks another memory fragment that helps break the blurred differences between my waking thoughts and actual dreams.

"I feel like I should know all of you." I point

jokingly as I approach the table.

"You think so?" Thumbs resumes the video playback while pocketing something I cannot identify. "You must be missing something."

"You all look like," I struggle with my words, rethinking the innuendo as I think of another comparison. "Are you all related?"

"Take a number." The stranger standing at the table turns away, refusing to look me in the eye.

"I mean," I chuckle in the confusion, pointing to the girl with orange hair. "Older sister, right?"

"See?" She sounds offended, trailing her sulking remarks. "I knew he was a loser." She turns away from the hologram, leaving the table.

I reach out and grab her arm, pulling her face into the light, revealing her locks of dirty blonde hair.

"You were at my apartment!"

Segments of memory that had been unraveled slowly twist together in a mosaic flash of self-realization. I remember her waking up in a daze outside my apartment and leaving without giving me a straight answer.

"What did you say about my wife?" My frustration turns sour.

"What are you talking about?" She raises her voice in a defensive tone.

"Stop lying!"

"Leave her alone!" Laci cries out. "She doesn't know!"

I grab the girl's arm, dragging her away from the suspended table.

"What's going on?" I state a serious inquiry to the adventurous youth.

"Hey --" her response scatters. "--that hurts!"

"Do I have to break your wrist to get a straight answer?" I pull the drawing of Sherianne from my pocket and shove it in her face. "Why were you at my place? When did you see my wife?"

"I already told you!" She sounds threatened, her voice cracking.

"Is your name, Anneli?"

"You're hurting me!"

Looking down, I can see that I am squeezing her wrist so tight her skin is turning white. I release her wrist and lower the drawing, moving for the open seat. My hands weigh me down like anchors as I set them on the suspended table. If I knew my wife, I would know what kind of trouble she would be in. With today's youth running around the city like there's no tomorrow to shield them from today, I feel as if time is running out.

"It's like I'm interrogating a ghost." Feeling like a beaten down man on the brink of a nervous breakdown, I stare at the drawing.

"What's that?" Laci leans across the table.

"A drawing." I reply without looking up at the curious young girl.

"She kind of looks like --" She looks up at the girl with orange hair while speaking to me, reading her queue to stop talking.

"Who does she look like?" My face stretches to full alert. "Do you know who this is?"

"Sorry," Laci straightens her posture. "My mistake. It's just so good. It looks like everyone, really."

Deflated, I turn toward the dancing crowd.

"Sherianne hated places like this," I start with a hint of denial in my voice. "Everything is backwards."

"Backwards?" Thumbs fusses. "People need a place to be backwards." He stops, looking over his shoulder at the mirrored wall and back across the table. "Straightens 'em out."

His focus switches from a glazed stare to a bored smirk that concludes with an activation code on his comp-uzync, which to him is both a remedy and destroyer of his full attention. The sound of random field entries leads me to doubt his capacity to hold a conversation. With a final key input delivered, he looks up at me, smiling through a hologram projection that quickly appears between us.

A cluster of female faces resides within the display. The dark colors in the projected image quickly dance into my tunnel vision, reverberating within me another level of synthetic music. A girl in the middle of the hologram reminds me of Sherianne and the way she moved when we were both young.

Sherianne, as I remember, is the only person I have truly loved. Having protested alongside thousands during the registration of neuro-metal implants, she proudly held her own against the Collar intervention.

Although my responsibility to SCS stood against everything she believed, our love for preservation proved superior. The girl in the projection resembles Sherianne in her younger form. Having been privileged to once share in Sherianne's childhood memories, I do not remember seeing her dance in such revealing public attire.

"How'd you get this?" I tilt my head with skepticism and squint at the near-transparent flicker. I reach out, passing my hand through the holographic display which distorts in zigzag patterns across the projected image.

"I have my sources," Thumbs looks at his comp-uzync, adjusting the contrast. "Ten fifteen over ten."

"Show me something recent." I approach the hologram. "Sherianne's my age."

"This was yesterday."

In a single moment, I realize that I am not looking for my wife, dancing her way into being crowned the city's most vivacious specimen. I realize by the disgusted look in Laci's frown that I am actually seeking out my surviving daughter.

"That's not his wife," Laci states, looking between me and Thumbs. "That's his daughter."

"-- And she gets a tip for every click," Thumbs adds.

"Like you could?" The girl with orange hair interjects. "You're an orphan too." She spits her words and swallows, wiping her mouth with her sleeve. "What did you do? Plan a heist?"

"Shut-up."

104

I think about baby Jessica and the ordeal she and her mother faced upon surviving the desert. I want to imagine my Jessica living without her mother in a place such as Thicket. She would have seen the city's authority at its worst, and although I would not want her growing up in the shadow of the government that betrayed her mother, I feel guilty for already judging her based on a single, skewed impression.

"I'm just going to say, your daughter --" Thumbs starts, sensing no one at the table is really listening to him.

Laci raises her hand, "-- is hot!"

Thumbs waves his hands in the air to encourage everyone nearby to laugh.

The footage of Jessica's dancing endeavor proves more than her sudden existence in the city. Her dance routine gives me a set of present-day steps that could narrow my search. I understand that Jessica is at the proper age for independence. She could be marked as a citizen, possibly adopted at an early age and able to live freely within Thicket, or she could be branded as an absconder, as her mother willingly chose over being controlled within the city.

The idea of Sherianne abandoning Jessica would never happen. She protected Jessica, with her own back to the threshold of a corrupt government that wants unconditional control and loyalty from its people.

Sherianne knew about the contracts each child would be forced to sign at birth, and she wanted a better life for our daughter. Each time I think upon my separated family, I envision them escaping Thicket on that warm day in April. As I picture them running, my heart rate increases. In my own insecurity, I always picture them losing the race, falling to the demands of Silver Collar zombies.

I sit in an invisible bubble of happiness and guilt, wishing my Imprint Drive was still promised to Arlita. Scanning the perimeter of the dance club, I continue the conversation with the rest of the table.

"Where's your father?"

"Everywhere, Digis," Thumbs drags the insult, smiling and wrapping his arm around Laci's shoulder.

I stand and quickly grab the table, stretching my arms to disrupt several integrated programs. "You think you have it all planned out." I pause and wait for Thumbs to speak.

"I --"

"-- I've seen the monitors."

The table starts to glitch, frustrated by my grip. I have Thumbs and Laci thinking about the Silver Collar Society and the millions of surveillance cameras lining the main avenues of Thicket. Laci ponders what may have been recorded when she thought she was alone, and Thumbs is intrigued about the range of control he could have at his command with the mass population in Thicket.

Sealing them with the impression that an authority

figure is shaking them down, I remain standing.

"You can't arrest me, Digis" he smirks. "So, what do you want?"

I glance at the table in the adjacent corral and notice them whispering.

"My name's Sunder. Quit the attitude," I snap.
"Bright and Sunny. Looking for something more perhaps," he offers his open hand as if conducting a business deal with Laci.
I return to my seat but look around the busy dance club. "I want what was taken from me," taking in the visual difference between dancers and diners, I notice Anneli is missing. "Where'd she go?"
"You can't tell people what to do, Sunny." Laci's eyes start to tighten as she pushes her chair away from the table and stands.

Struggling to agree with the terms that somehow make sense, I think about my wife and daughter, and I try to imagine the danger they have already faced. Unable to force anyone to get a straight answer, I feel trapped at the beginning with no way to progress. A portion of my sanity includes believing my family is alive, but without knowing their whereabouts, my memory of their happiness is threatened.

Near the front of the club, I spot the waitress with florescent blue hair leaning over a table, conducting another transaction with its patrons. An elderly man sits comfortably in the company of several young women, attracted to the regal shine of his Silver Collar.

As the music of the repetitive generation continues into the early hours of the morning, I think about the about the stranger in my apartment.

Worrying about the Silver Collar Society and the reason they have for monitoring me is enough to drive any citizen crazy. What is it about Anneli and the connection she could have to my family?

While leaving the East Sector Club, I realize something important. I was never cool. I never have been special. I am simply average. I may no longer be licensed as a specialist or be able to classify myself as an engineer or give myself the title of husband; I did remember something else important. I will always be a father.

Chapter 7

Every Adverse

..

"No servant can serve two masters, for either he will hate the one and love the other, or he will be devoted to the one and despise the other. You cannot serve God and money."

Luke 16:13

..

On the streets outside the East Sector Club, the mood is different from every other sector. All is quiet, comparably. As the sun rises and the ruckus of the marketplace stirs, I hear the selling sounds of controlled relief. The glass advertisement boards flicker words in bold print over thousands of commuters. As if ordered with a type of visual aid to enjoy the start of my day, I am forced to follow SCS rules to respect my neighbor. Like every citizen in Thicket, who must earn the right to live here, I am told to behave.

The warmth of the city street is vital to the survival of humanity and the Silver Collar Society provides the digital circuitry to power the neuro-metal pavement. The surface acts as an insulator in the winter and conditioner in the summer, requiring massive amounts of electricity. A sufficient power station, designed and installed by SCS engineers, generates the voltage from the dry riverbed directly below the city's foundation.

On both sides of my path, people sleep on the heated streets. Vendors along the edge, display their hand-made merchandise in piles and grids at their feet. Thousands of desperate people sell hand-stitched fabrics that can only be used inside the city. While I pass up their tempting offers, wondering what the fabrics are woven from, I rub my balding head and trek deeper into the marketplace where the smell of a bountiful feast lures the city's walking population.

The animals of the old world cannot survive today. The city is not designed to support the ecological need of both human and animal. Except for the aroma of a home cooked meal that emanates from steam vents between each marketplace intersection, animal sustenance does not exist, yet the people of Thicket have grown accustomed to the artificial smell of bacon and barbecue.

The bulk of Thicket's population must rely on three pills a day, followed by a digestible marble before bed. My entire diet is mandated, including flavored protein drinks of 200ml marbles that are distilled from a mixture of cauliflower and bio-luminescent algae. Artificial colors and flavors are added to help us accept the fact that normal food is a thing of the past. I like to think that Cherry Red is my favorite.

As I knew would happen, the breakfast bell rings in my head and my stomach rumbles. Now would be the moment my body demands a pill. My C-Tab supply usually keeps my mind in check and satisfies my hunger, but missing a pill means less energy, poor decision-making skills, and a variety of other impairments that will eventually lead to malnutrition and starvation.

"Presses!" One vendor exclaims.

"Marbles. Get third free!" Another vendor rivals.

"Collar special! Presses and marbles! Special for Collars!" A third vendor invites.

My choices continue for as far as the marketplace perfumes. When the people of Thicket reinvented the luxury of corrupted currency, they invested in rival dispensers of the same government issued nutrition package. As one vendor tries to outsell his neighbor, I remember the simple spite of stores that existed merely to compete against another service, catering to the same clientele. Each vendor bares a greedier smile in their sale than the previous one I pass along the way.

"Fantastic presses!" One vendor tries to persuade.

"Know the difference! Buy from me!" An elder vendor tries to speak over everyone else.

"Can I get your presses in cherry?" I mock the old man's confidence.

"Maybe," he breathes in. "These presses won't smell like the shoveled carcasses of a thousand vermin."

This is not the first time I have heard this vendor's opening line to closing a sale. But for the first time I consider his service on the streets of Thicket to be valuable. As many would try to cheat their way into acquiring more credit through some planned glitch in their transaction drive, I settle on a sure sale to keep me alive.

"Tell me, Uni. How does SCS cook the vermin?" I

squat down to admire the other artifacts for sale at his kiosk.

"They send children --" Uni speaks to me as well as those wandering by his venue. "-- with suits and shovels. Big shovels. Bigger than shoulders." He begins licking the air as if an invisible salt block sits on his collarbone.

Uni is short for acting unique, and the children of Thicket gave this old vendor such a nickname for his fictitious rants of underground furnaces accompanied by the occasional habit of unrolling his tongue during a conversation. Uni's behavior never brings him trouble, nor does it bestow upon him any luck. I see Uni as a restructured child, lost in the body of a crumbing adult, and on the last leg for being a threat.

His full beard sways in the wind, complimenting the loose silver locks of his long, unkempt mane. Animated with course eyebrows of nearly the same length, Uni's weathered face reveals more than a few prominent laugh lines. His dementia-driven appearance could be his best disguise.

Selfish shoppers ignore Uni on their way through the North Beta Sector and arrogant hypocrites avoid him on their way to the city's cathedral. To these patrons of Thicket, Uni sells nothing but useless stories that could possibly be used to scare young children into obeying their parents.

"Black skin. Black vermin with --" Uni gazes up into the dawning sky while spitting. "-- pink lips. Black box. Gray farm. Black and Silver. Silver Collar.

112

Copied soul. Soul forever --" he rambles on, unaware to what he is saying.

"Wait. Go back. What black box?" I turn up, intrigued by his one-sided dialogue.

Thinking Uni overheard part of some important conversation, I want to believe his regurgitated words are the recipe of some master plan. What may have been whispering rambles inside of Uni's thought chamber could be translated into the string of details that match the occurrences to my weekday of trouble.

"Pink lips after SCS." Uni's gaze returns to the streets in a blush.

"Pink lips?" I squint as my eyes connect with him.

"Farm lips." Uni starts to lick the air, turning to face the invisible salt block that now sits on his other shoulder.

"Can you show me this farm?" I stand.

"Desert vermin fear the farm. Absconders run the farm. Father knows the prophecy." Uni quickly turns away from me as if he has said too much.

"Whose father?" I ask, eager to know more. "Yours?"

Uni starts vigorously rubbing his face and the top of his head as if he is being attacked by a swarm of accusations. A squeak emanates from within, rearranging Uni's entire vocabulary, processing his voice like the screams of either a scared rodent or an ill-oiled hinge.

"I'll trade you." I reach into my desert suit and pull out the cylindrical container.

Uni turns on the ball of his foot, grinning with both hands over his crooked smile that surfaces for the first sale in a long time. Having the reputation of scaring his customers, Uni contributes his lack of funds to the sight of his artificial body. Selling his body parts for more than enough credit to live forever, Uni carries on making a living.

His makeshift venue is no more than a few handmade desk ornaments and pieces of reconstructed metal that double as a preconditioned art project. His available merchandise sits on the city's street as does the hundreds of others in this sector of the marketplace that try to keep capitalism alive. Uni picks up a large box off the pavement, opening it as quickly as he can, and seems to dive face first into its open lid.

Uni is beyond excited, grabbing more than a handful of little gray oval presses. He closes the box and sets it down with the other hand while trying to balance the excessive number of pills he withdrew. With both hands as a dedicated serving tray, he offers the mound of synthetic nutrition to me.

"Well," I ponder. "I guess I'll take this one." I reach for a random pill near the edge of the pile.
"Not that one." Uni jerks his neck, swatting with his eyes.
"Right," I start, a little confused. "I meant this one." My hand changes direction.
"No, not that one." Uni swats with his eyes again.
"Then which one, Uni? They're all the same." I retract my hand.

"Hard to say," he looks down at the presses in both hands. "But they've been cleaned." Uni leans closer and breathes in. "They don't smell."

"Alright." I feel like I have had enough of Uni's games. "Do you want to trade or not?"

Uni takes my negative review as a challenge, and as if asserting his presence as my elder, he lowers his voice, looking directly into my eyes.

"You're taking one now."

Over the years, Uni's persuasive gestures have become depressing. His empathetic stare remains fixed as he drops the lot in his hands, except for two. More than three dozen pressed pills bounce off folds in his attire and disperse across the tiny corner of the marketplace. Uni holds both identical presses up to eye-level where they serve as an operator between offended customer and disgruntled clerk.

"This one is for now." Uni holds up his right hand, and then his left. "This one for passage."

"I only want one, Uni." I reach for his left hand.

"It's not up to you." Uni shoves both pills into my empty palm. "Just remember," he encroaches with bright, dilated pupils. "The Suite is no place for a child. There's a plague on humanity. Like the painted rock under the violet ultra, the creature will appear unique." He breaks his stare, taking a step back and rubbing his eyes.

"Like I need more desert rocks," I remark quietly.

With the awkward rubbing over, I watch Uni hunch

115

down onto his knees to pick up the scattered presses. Nearby shoppers pay extra attention to his surrounding misfortune. Children who wander the marketplace unsupervised stop only to swipe a press or two while Uni is busy with our sale. He tries to stop one child who grabs a handful but falls backwards onto the neuro-metal pavement in a heavy collapse.

I do not consider it my responsibility to curb an adolescent lawbreaker. I could grab one by the elbow and force out an apology, but I do not feel any obligation to uphold the law. If the Silver Collar Society does not look out for my safety and well-being, why should I enforce any ordinance of civil obedience?

"I despise children," Uni mumbles as he reaches for the last of his stray presses.

I cannot settle on agreeing with Uni, but I feel compelled to respect his verbal assertion. Maybe he is wasting his time as a bitter man. With all the work he had done to repair his body, some would find it difficult to still consider him human. The words I want to say are clashed together, rolling around like thousands of marbles in my mind. Before I can speak, I hear a voice that I may never be able to trust.

"I wouldn't do that," Someone points to my mouth as I ingest a pill.
"How's that?" I swallow and glance down at Uni who is preoccupied with moving his collection of pressed pills back into his box.
"That's how they track you." She glances at the

116

second press in my hand. "You like being watched?"

"Right." I look off into the distance. "Now, you're following me? I thought you didn't speak."

"Still --" She sounds convinced that I set the entire interrogation scene in motion but then continues as if she has quickly forgotten about being mad. "Are you really going to take those things?"

"Yup," I mockingly smile, depositing the second press into my cylindrical container. "Vermin-free."

The thought of shoveling vermin starts to turn her stomach, as the girl with orange hair remembers scavenging with a shovel twice the size of her chest. She squats down to help Uni gather the few remaining presses, handing him all that she collects. She glances at me with a preview to cringing as if I am responsible for allowing her to taste actual vermin.

"Am I supposed to feel sorry, or guilty for being hungry?" I look down on her sulking with a dusting of both my hands.

"You never worked underground," she looks up, sneering. "How would you know?"

I would know. I remember the absconder camps outside the city that housed the hundreds of outcast families, many of whom worked underground and socialized with those people who were as important to me as they are to her.

"Besides, he's right about the Suite," she falters, returning to Uni's aid.

"The Suite Oasis?" I feel led.

"Far from curious ears. No place for a child."

117

I find myself unable to respond, thinking about my wife and the life she chose to live. Sherianne, like the other absconders in her camp, survived the desert by scavenging the land of anything valuable. Because of the neuro-metal lining her suit, Sherianne was able to function in the extreme.

Like many absconders, this stranger has her own desert suit that looks like my own. Knowing about the harsh reality of the desert, I contemplate the simple act of walking a tour against the wasteland winds and wild weather. As truth comes to understanding the trial and mortal error of life on such forsaken land, I chew on my tongue over sounding foolish.

Her tears seem held back, and if given the appropriate shoulder, she could cry forever. She looks up at me as she slowly stands.

"Have you ever had to make a choice that could either make or break your world, and still affect everyone else?" She moves in closer. "You should have known better."

"Why are you here?" My eyes pan the roots of her orange hair until I see a trace of brown.

"Your name's Oscar, right?" She looks at me after admiring Uni's merchandise.

"Yeah? How did you know that?"

Her face softens as she touches Uni's shoulder. She moves around him and quietly scoops up a pair of desert boots that he has for sale. Dropping her smile, she picks up a second pair and starts walking away, being careful to not be seen. With Uni distracted, I march after her.

"Who are you?"

"Does it really matter?" She leads me into the crowd.

"Then why should I care?" I sound unsure as to why I am following her. "I already have a life." I feel ready to walk in the other direction.

"We can't always get what we want." She glances back before turning a corner. "He has your cube."

Aware of my nightmares, I follow her through the marketplace but fall into confusion over her mission. As my selfish desires start to question her knowledge of the cube, I watch her openly swing the pair of desert boots in her hands, wondering why she needs a second pair.

"Who? Thumbs?" I feel compelled to stop our venture until I get a direct answer.

"Wait -- What?" She chuckles, sure of his reputation. "No." She keeps moving in the same direction, hoping to challenge my curiosity. "Father wouldn't allow that."

As we continue walking, now in silence, I think of my daughter and the way she would have referred to me as Father. I remember the ways Jessica's tiny hands held onto my forefinger as I carried her. Although I never got to hear her first words, I always believed Jessica would have developed into a strong and confident woman, just as this stranger escorting a man two and a half times her age.

"What does your father have to do with me?"

"He said you helped make him, I don't know --" She holds the boots in the air as if she has no idea.

She stops, looking up at the Alpha and Beta Wings of Thicket's Medical Sector. As her mind starts to wander, I think of the unlisted market that helped to furnish my elaborate apartment. With the Silver Collar Society following my every move, there is no easy way for me to conduct business.

"He knows you can't save him, so what's the point, right?" She glances back at me with a sense of uneasiness.

"What?" I feel her crying for helping.

She gazes up at the Medical Tower where thousands of reinforced windows exhibit medical experiments and recovering adjustments. Each room in the Medical Tower is equipped to reduce a patient's healing time by half. Her eyes fall but she cannot hide her emotions.

"Is that why you settled?" I point to her wrist.

"I didn't have a choice." She glances down an alleyway, sounding impatient, yet depressed. "Nobody knows who I am."

"And I do?" My words come out surprisingly calm.

"I kind of thought you would. I mean, you're a doctor, right?"

I think about all the people who have come to me for help and about all the ones I must turn away because of the reputation I need to protect. I understand her need for medical attention, but I have a gut feeling that there is something she is not telling me.

If there is an ailment she suffers from, I am unaware of her symptoms. Her health must not be important to her since she is failing to seek the proper help. I have always wondered what absconders in the city do when faced with a matter of life or death. I figured a scavenger of the desert would know where to go and what to do, but now, I guess I am wrong.

"Not anymore. I --" I begin sympathetically. "I just know how to point people in the other direction."

She looks around, wondering if we are being watched. The large medical buildings will not protect us from old debts or classified stress.

"You know what? Never mind." She sounds impatient, as if my ignorance is wasting her time. "I can manage to keep myself alive."
"Then, if you really don't need me, I'm going this way." My sarcasm allows my steps to take me in another direction.
"Brought on by selfish acts," she murmurs.

As the young absconder starts walking again, leaving the birthing shadow of the Medical Tower, my mind starts to flicker. I remember Sherianne getting mad at me for not wanting to stay with her as she settled in her new home outside Thicket. She told me my decision was brought on by selfish acts. Unable to ignore the coincidence, I turn and walk after her as she approaches the edge of the Medical Sector and the entry-port to the rocky wasteland.

"What did you just say?" I reach out and grab her arm.

"You're selfish." She pulls her arm free.

"You're not being straight with me." I point at her face, stepping back from the entry-port. "Why should I believe you? What if I go home, ignore you like everyone else?"

"Because --"

"Because what? You know something I don't? You know where she is? You know why she's been gone all this time and refused to drop me a line?" My hands go up with my temper. "What is it? Is she spelunking and unable to find her way home? At least that would be something --" I rant, unwilling to hear her.

"Because!"

She pulls on a large lever to the circular port.

"Jessica's going to die."

The citizens of the North Alpha and Beta Sectors live in the cleanest portion of Thicket. Most would believe the residential apartments surrounding the Medical Sector are owned by the upper class and citizens involved in the Silver Collar Society.

The northern edge of the marketplace is considered by most to be the end of the road, but I feel I am being led in a direction that requires a checkpoint. Twisting gears and harmonious chirps of electricity resonate from within the walls of reseeded steel. The entry-port's pressurized release sends a gust of white steam in our direction.

The outside air smells burnt. What looks to be a cave-in of rubble and rot is a ladder to an endless desert of unbelievable sandstorms, crashing into one another like tornadoes of dirt and grime. Beyond the walls of the Hetch Hetchy Valley, absconders are home.

"You don't have to follow me." She drops the pair of boots in front of me and pulls up the hood that laid zippered under the folds in her desert suit. She takes a step outside, glancing back before wandering off.

If I had a choice, I would remain within the city limits and let her wander back to her father, but I must think of my daughter. I need to make sure she's okay, so I can be okay. Instead of turning around and disappearing back into the marketplace, I pick up the pair of boots and slip them on. I unfold the hood to my own desert suit and tighten the neuro-metal fabric around my face. Taking a deep breath, I step through the entry-port just as the circular hatch closes behind me with a loud, pressurized seal.

Chapter 8

Layers in Dirt

..

"And no wonder, for even Satan disguises himself as an angel of light."

2 Corinthians 11:14

..

The desert wind smothers my face as a strange teenage girl leads me through the rugged landscape. Battling against the heat that surrounds each step, the rocks and sand release the scent of tepid decay. There are no trees to shelter us from the morning sun. No bodies of water to cross. The land surrounding Thicket is dead.

The darker stained sky, although dense and receptive to solar radiation, does not aid us in the extreme fluctuation in temperature. At the top of what looks like a botched cave-in, I look to the west and ignorantly smile at an even spread of clouds. I like to think that the world is not in complete peril when every few days, the weather breaks its threshold.

She turns with a hand shading her eyes, "We're heading east!" Her voice crashes in the wind.

"East?" I shade my eyes, wondering if the absconder camp in the same direction is still occupied.

"Don't look surprised --" she walks past me but looks back. "-- and don't fall behind."

Rain clouds appear in the west, marking the occasion with an encroaching layer of acidic fog. The desert suit I wear can protect me from most of nature's updated elements, but not all of them.

Behind the walls of Thicket, we would be safe. A large, ionized vent would shield us from this corrosive storm. Now that I am far from the comfort of Thicket's safety, I must deal with this deadly fog in my own way. Raised by refugees and protesters still living outside the city, someone needs takes charge on which way to go.

For several hours we hike to the nearest absconder camp. Marching up hills and around large boulders. We cross old highways that are no longer in service and illegible road signs that can barely stand on their own. The sight of camp appears on the horizon.

"Don't talk to anyone." She watches me as we approach the camp. "These people don't want your help."

I scan the perimeter of the camp, identifying shelters made of a steel, copper, and zinc. Their irregular shapes outline the poverty that should no longer exist in the world but as I search for anyone who may be able to help, I am quick to assume that this camp is dead. While the locals call this part of the mountain ridge, Paiute, the flagpole at the center of camp identifies it as Crowchest. I feel reminded of Sherianne's decision to raise our daughter in a community like this one without the help of the Silver Collar Society.

The camp is clustered closely together, leaving no

room for additional structures. I approach one home nearest the flagpole and slowly open the door that is cut from a single piece of metal. The interior walls look like shackled pieces of steel and large eroded stones, removed from a dry riverbed to accent each corner. I am inspecting a metal canister on a nearby shelf when I notice her outside walking by impatiently.

"Where is everyone?" She sticks her head through the open doorways of several homes. "Their stuff's still here."

"I know this camp." As I walk outside, I feel as though my voice cannot be heard over the wind battering a dozen shingled structures. "You can't find this place with an old-fashioned compass."

"I'm sure." She does not sound impressed, seeming distracted by the camp's desertion.

"It's the reverse in polarity. If you headed north on a compass, it would send you in the opposite direction. My wife brought our daughter here. It wasn't safe in the city."

She reaches for a broken hydro-generator that rests upside down. As I join her, I help her turn the generator on its side.

"Safe for you, but not for them." She ignores my attempt to help.

"It's not that simple." I notice her face is sweating. "I risked everything to be with her. It wasn't easy for me." I remove a side panel of the generator to reveal a circuit board of wires and small tubes. The gears in my head start to turn.

"You abandoned them." She stands, stepping away

126

from the broken machine.

"I didn't have a choice." I bury my shame in the generator's open compartment.

She brushes off a layer of sand that has accumulated on her sweaty cheeks, tightening her hood in frustration.

"Someone told SCS about this place."

"Are you accusing me?" I look up.

"Look at this place!" She stretches her arms out and looks around. "There's nothing left!"

"How is this my fault? I loved my family. I did everything I could to make sure they had a life." I push my finger into my open palm.

"Not everything." She crosses her arms in disappointment, returning her stare to the horizon.

The wind starts to pick up speed. She reaches into one of her large pockets and retrieves a handful of Cau-li presses. She offers her closed hand to me.

"Put these in your bottle."

"Did you take these from Uni?" I feel torn accepting her gift.

"Does it matter?"

"I think it should," I open my container and deposit the presses. "Everyone should be held accountable."

"Hypocrite."

"Why are you so angry with me?"

With her back to me, she stands at the edge of a low-lying cliff. Watching the horizon, she spots the approaching storm. I return my focus to the hydro-generator on its side. I plug and unplug wires and rearrange several tubes until the device begins to hum. I replace the side panel and turn the generator upright.

"I don't know why you're mad at me, I don't even know your name. I protected my family the only way I knew how."

Shielding her face from the chocking gust, she keeps silent.

"I'm not going to let Jessica die." I pick up the hydro-generator that is now fully functional and get to my feet. "Are we clear?"

She steps down from the edge of the cliff and turns toward a mountain ridge on the opposite side of the camp, "We need to hurry."

She treks up the mountainside to the entrance of a cave. Although the mouth of the cave is no bigger than an entry-port in the city, the belly of the cave is ideal for sheltering us from the storm. Leading the way, she instructs me to watch my step around stalagmites that sharpen near my waist.

"We'll wait for the storm to pass." She takes a seat near a rounded boulder.
"How long will that take?" I stand close to the light of the entrance.
"Maybe a few hours," she makes herself comfortable by laying on her back. "You got somewhere to be?"

The average absconder has seen their share of acidic storms and has survived the worst by learning from those who failed to heed proper advice. Once the acidic clouds leave the area, the ground will still be covered in puddles, cavities in stone. Walking at night with a randomized field of acidic ponds is not the easiest obstacle to maneuver, even for those skilled at territory warfare. She would do as she always did when faced with these circumstances. Even if I am willing to leave on my own, the guilt of abandoning my daughter will force me to return and wait until the sun evaporates all evidence of the storm.

As She loosens her desert suit hood, she looks around the cave, squinting at anything the light touches. She catches sight of a couple of words, carved into the wall near a large stalagmite.

"Stay natural," she reads aloud.

Hearing her say those words catches my attention. It makes me think of Sherianne and way we first met. As my mind starts to wander, gladly accepting the reminiscence of my lost love, her commentary goes wild.

"Stay natural? What the hell does that even mean?" She tightens her brow, criticizing the line of graffiti for its misleading message. "Are we farmers?"

While I feel amused, I keep silent. I set the hydro-generator on the floor of the cave and watch the approaching cloud. Lightning strikes in the distance, illuminating the evening sky with a sudden burst of electricity. The absconders who lived here could protect themselves from the acidic storms, but they failed in fleeing the authority of the Silver Collar Society. The storm gathers in heavier patches over the camp, raining in larger segments. Lightning flashes again, hitting the floor of the cave. I flinch as sparks surround my feet.

"We should move to the back of the cave," I reach for the hydro-generator.
"What are you talking about?" She sounds groggy.

I grab her arm, pulling her away from the mouth of the cave. She tears herself away from my hold and finds another comfortable spot to lay.

"You should get some sleep." She tries to sound invincible.
"What about you?"
"Don't worry about me. Nobody does."

She ignores me and rolls onto her side. I lean back against the cave wall and close my eyes, listening to the rain and hoping my dilemma will soon fade into the darkness. Against the hissing wind of the cave, I hear a voice.

"My name's Shantelle."

After several hours, the heavy beads of the storm slow to a trickle and eventually cease to fall. I fall asleep in the confidence of the mountain's solid structure while Shantelle now patrols the entrance, unable to find sleep.

In the blanket of my dreams, I find myself at the base of a large solitary tree that looks to have been torched by fire but then reinforced with a change of heart.

I hear a voice in the wind.

I reach for the branch of the tree, a nervous voice calls from the ground. Shantelle is there, calling for me to climb back down before something bad happens.

Instead of following her worried request, I climb higher. The same voice in the wind finds me.

An approaching storm picks up in speed and the tree begins to disintegrate, withering away like grains of sand in the wind.

Suddenly, I find myself standing on the ground and Shantelle is the one climbing the tree. Appearing beside me is a figure cloaked in darkness, donning a large gas mask with an illuminated airway, bathed in a red halo, holding the comp-ucube, inviting me to look inside.

I desperately want to look inside but wait for the voice in the wind.

The tree trunk cracks and quickly disappears, leaving Shantelle suspended in the sky without an anchor. She screams for her father and falls.

I lunge forward in a panic, hoping to catch her, but

feel dragged down. The quicker I run, the faster she plummets to the hard ground below.

The next morning, the sun begins its day by evaporating the many large puddles of acidic moisture from the ground. I am the first to wake in a violent shake, recalling a dream that includes Shantelle, a heavy storm, and a burnt tree. I feel as though I am living out the shadow of someone's dream, while always looking for another hand to hold. I dream where every touch feels like gold to me. As I get to my feet, I look toward the entrance of the cave and out over the campsite that survived another fierce storm. I move to Shantelle who lays motionless from her night's sleep.

"Shantelle? Wake-up. The storm's over." I shake her arm.

Shantelle's eyes flicker as she begins to wake. Instead of greeting me with a reasonable welcome, or an anticipated shove of my heavy form away from her vast personal space, she coughs continuously. leading to the expulsion of her stomach's contents. I stand back, giving her enough room to breathe.

"Are you alright?" I reach for the hydro-generator, filling a collapsible container that I carry in my desert suit. "Here, drink this." I reach for Shantelle's shoulder and hand her the cup of water.
"I -- I don't know." Shantelle takes a sip of the water but is unable to swallow. She coughs and vomits again. "It's happening again."
"You really are sick."

"You think?" she wipes the saliva that has accumulated in the corner of her mouth.

"Well, I can't be sure." I help her stand, noticing a dark red mark on her shoulder that looks swollen. "When did you get that?" I point to the part of her skin that looks like a recent bite mark.

"That?" She looks at her shoulder, quickly looking away as if she does not care. "I don't know. I've had that for a while." She rubs her shoulder, worsening the expression of discomfort on her face while showing off her tolerance to pain.

"It looks infected." I touch the surrounding area of the wound which is just as sensitive. "We need to get that covered."

"We don't need to do anything." She pushes my hand away and pulls a square of fabric from her pocket.

Shantelle tears the fabric into two pieces and dowses them with water from the hydro-generator. As she unravels the first piece, I take the second strip of fabric and tie it around her shoulder.

"What the hell --" She pulls her shoulder back in pain.

"You'll thank me."

"Yeah? And what about you?" She tightens the first piece of wet fabric around her face.

As soon as Shantelle holds the filter to her face, her breathing seems to improve. She no longer smells the heat in the air, or the aroma of wildfires that seem beyond control. Once we leave the cave and the absconder camp in the distance, Shantelle begins to feel better. She holds her head up as she tightens the hood around her face. Soon she can walk on her own.

"There must have been something in that cave." I look back at the horizon before the camp disappears behind another mountain.

Particles of heavy dirt, along with both the rotten and rusted bits of the old world, ride the storm throughout the day. I can smell blood and metal in the air among the swept-up clouds of sand, and I can barely distinguish Shantelle's silhouette in the leading distance. I move cautiously through the desert fog, covering the narrow opening in my hood from any intrusion. Shantelle moves like she is coated in repellent, not phased from anything wrong with the state of the world.

As I struggle to keep my pace up, I watch Shantelle march with confidence, wondering how my daughter could have survived the desert. If Shantelle can figure a way, so could Jessica. I'd like to imagine Jessica turned out as strong as her mother, if not stronger. I want to believe everything was fine when I left their camp all those years ago.

Shantelle easily maneuvers around large obstacles in the ground by following a path that is familiar to her. She leads me through a graveyard of toppled automobiles, an asphalt sea of mangled shopping carts, and a mountain of rubble that looks to contain the pieces of an entire neighborhood.

"There! You see that?" Shantelle stops and points to

a tornado in the dirt.

"See what?" I join her in looking. "The desert tornado?"

"No," she turns in an impatient tone. "The tower! The antenna!"

I squint my eyes but see only a twisting symphony of dirt. "I don't see a tower. Are you sure you're okay?"

"The tall silver thing --" Shantelle quickly checks behind her, now seeing dirt devils in peripherals. "I thought I saw the lookout point." She looks around, loosening her hood. "We must have passed it."

A majority of the wasteland surrounding the city seems cleaner than the outlining mountain ranges. Without trees, shrubs, or any kind of foliage, the unending horizon blends with the uneasy smell of the dead. My vision narrows the longer I walk, catching the sun's rays without somewhere to stare. I can barely see Shantelle, who continues her march only a few meters ahead.

The burning smell of a scorched earth lingers over every stone and every low-lying mound of hardened clay. Even the sand I pass seems to retain the essence of a pebble that lost its way home. A sort of poetic atmosphere triggers my memory over a time that belongs to me and my family.

I remember hearing about the revolution on Paiute Mountain. Sherianne had developed a reputation for voicing her opinions against neuro-metal implants. Jessica was wrapped in a neuro-metal garment to shield her from the desert winds. The forsaken ambiance of the wastelands brings tears to my troubled past, as does the unrelenting heat that makes my eyes burn. Without a proper face mask, I could suffer a heat stroke or go blind.

From Thicket, we walk for nearly 16 hours beyond the mountains of crumbled bricks and folded steel, to the western shore of the formerly great, Lake Mono. Branded as a haven for those needing help, Lake Mono is now home to the Suite Oasis.

Before the thought of collapsing crosses my mind, Shantelle calls to me.

"We're almost there!" She shouts to be heard over the wind. "I'm going to warn you!"
"Yeah?" I try my best to listen.
"Don't run," she pauses, looking forward at the badly damaged building in the distance. "He's not going to kill you! Got it?"
"What?" The only words I hear are KILL and YOU.
"Got it?"
"What?" I shield my eyes, unable to get a straight answer.

Against the backdrop of a dry lakebed, I spot a building that resembles our sanctuary. The closer we get, the more I sense the structure is identical to the surface of Thicket's narrow streets, only covered in desert decor. The neuro-metal shelter contains its own electromagnetic pulse, and with each step Shantelle and I take toward the building's exterior, the electronic buzz in the wind grows louder.

The Suite's entry-port, somewhat hidden by the desert's erosion, looks like the tens of thousands installed all over Thicket. The circular frame seems badly worn, as if someone once tried to break in. I walk up to the structure and rub its surface that crumbles like chalk. This entry-port may have been the very first, eagerly developed as a substantial portal, and used as a barrier between the Silver Collar Society and the untrustworthy absconders of the wasteland.

"This looks easy," I offer my cynicism, assuming the same about all entry-ports.

"It is," Shantelle approaches the building and reveals a hidden a metal plate. "Just not for you."

Shantelle places her open palm on a handprint scanner and the entry-port creaks as internal mechanics rotate the door open. The inside of the neuro-metal building houses several large filtration devices, each with a metallic bin connected to a processing machine leading toward the city's water supply. The equipment operates at a decibel lower than the desert winds making our entrance more welcoming.

The floor of the building is slanted, leading to a path deep underground. From first impressions, the mechanics of the room is a litter of odd angles and shapes of scrap metal, alongside tools that look recently handled. On one side of the room, a dark hooded figure drops an unlit welding torch with a loud clang when he notices us emerge from behind one of the working extractors.

"You," the hooded absconder approaches, almost as if floating over his scattered belongings. "You must be Sunder." His electronic voice seems to sneer as he pronounces my name. He sounds like he does not belong this far above ground.

"Perhaps," I grow hesitant, shifting my eyes between Shantelle and the absconder cloaked in his own shadow.

"I've heard so much already," The absconder expresses his words with long sleeves covering his hands. "Do you know the tale of the man who tried to live forever?"

"Rings a bell," I answer with a quick glance around the workshop.

The absconder turns and squats over a small mound of neuro-metal fragments where hidden from my view he selects a piece of a hardened circuit board. Standing, at best as a hunchback, he turns to me and flicks the chunk of neuro-metal.

"Swallow that," he points to the piece I catch.

I tumble the circuit board between my fingers and notice how it tickles the implant in my arm. I look up at the absconder who hides his face well in the barely lit room. Deep in the hood of his robe, which seems to be made primarily from compressed human hair, his features are cased in shadow. When I search for the eyes to match the voice, I get the feeling I am looking at more fragments of neuro-metal.

"Alright," I feel like I have had enough. "What's going on?" I toss the piece of neuro-metal to the ground and hold my arms out.

"You're the father, aren't you?" The absconder points with his sleeve, revealing a finger that looks to be dipped in neuro-metal. "She's here, you know. Your daughter?"

I feel paralyzed as I watch him turn away.

"Shantelle here --" gesturing for her to leave through an entry-port on the other side of the room. "-- has been trying to keep her alive."

"She's what?" I confusingly watch Shantelle leave.

The absconder silently approaches the sealed entry-port, flipping back his long sleeves. He drags his fingertips against the surface, scratching the reseeded steel.

"Have you ever injected neuro-metal directly into bone marrow?" He moves his hand in a circle, leaving deep grooves in the entry-port.

"What --" I squint while trying to process his question. "Why? Even if I did, I wouldn't survive."

"Oh, I know."

He turns and rushes toward me, grabbing me by the throat.

His hood falls to reveal a bald head, coated in neuro-metal, and covered in cracks as would be a human skull. The hardened black sludge that coats his fingers and wrists extends up both arms, across his chest, and between his shoulder blades. His ears look to be molded to the side of his face while his nose sinks in flush with his brow. I look down and see that in between his limbs and movable joints, the neuro-metal has wrinkles, looking like a rubber callus over his normal epidermis.

"Of all the people in Thicket, I'd expect you to know." He looks at me with eyes that seem to be burning off electricity from an overloading source.

I cannot help but feel scared, lost in my own mind like a child without a guardian. I feel my airways closing, being crushed by hands that could easily break my neck. Flooded by the fear of humanity's mistake, my senses are overpowered by the product of evil. I see a manifestation of man in the mask of technology. I may very well be looking at the man who tried to live forever.

At first, I was at a loss of words, juggling my emotions like a partially digested meal on its way up. Now I have to blink several times, to breathe and understand what is happening. Something bubbles out from my mouth, and to my amazement, they are words that I believe to be true.

"Expect?" I try to inhale. "Nobody expects anymore."

Suddenly, he releases me and lets me fall to the ground.

I back away from the absconder and crawl toward an ionizing pump.

"It used to be that people expected the world to end." He watches me holding my neck and approaches the large device from the other side.

I look up and see a series of visible pumps circulate a continual supply of brown liquid into a collection chamber before disappearing into the next room.

"People expect their government to save them from every possible disaster. Now," he points to the viewing window of the churned waste. "We're trying to live forever on our own."

Not able to speak, I watch him move toward the scattered equipment as if disregarding my presence or the pain I feel. Ignoring any empathy, he reaches down to move a socket wrench. Then after lifting a plank of metal and pushing it to the side, he examines the unlit welding torch.

"Youth has its advantages. Don't you agree?" The absconder looks up, pulling his hood back over his face. "Before I was exiled, the people of Thicket loved me." He drops the welding torch for a screwdriver. "The people looked up to me. I was the son of an important man." He stands, gripping the screwdriver in my direction. "Now, they call me, Father. Father Khristoff."

The absconder offers his name, which in turn makes me remember. The talk with Arlita seems more important now. A written page of history is mere text to someone like me, while to Arlita and Father Khristoff, the past is still alive. Having survived being escorted to

141

a region far outside the city, Khristoff never forgot how those who he thought were on his side left him to the wastelands for speaking his mind.

"You're that Dakya kid." I sit up.

Khristoff stares, shaking me with the size of his glowing eyes. "There was a time when people called me, Loy. Even my own father, at one point, respected me."

There is a part of me that sympathizes with Khristoff. In his former life, Loy would have enthusiastically introduced himself to every person in the room. Before injecting neuro-metal in the bone marrow of both arms and spinal cord, Loy would have horded his own supply of Cau-li to feed his neighbor. The young boy who grew up as Loy Dakya, only son to a famous neurological surgeon, abandoned the identity of his past. To survive the extremity of the wastelands and preserve the future of his destiny, Loy created a creature that the people of Thicket have now come to fear.

"Why stay here?" I look around the room again, correcting my first impression about the smell. "What could you possibly get out here?" I glance at the scattered tools over sheets of metal.

"My children." Khristoff lays his elongated neuro-metal fingers on a compression engine, jolting the machine into a rumble with a tiny spark. "I send them out to reap the land."

"With what, large shovels?" I rub my neck, trying to hide my sarcasm.

Khristoff smiles, hiding a memory that seems fresh in his mind.

"Have you ever seen a bat devour a bat?" Khristoff calmly twists the screwdriver into the side of the engine.

I imagine myself exploring the campsite cavern where bats contribute to the putrid smell. Because of their ravenous appetites and the basic assertion to survive, they have surrounded the city of Thicket.

"I never figured bats for cannibals." Not wanting to indulge his fantasy, I sense I am learning something new.

"Savages." He digs the screwdriver into a crevice on the engine, lifting a large panel. "A sight like you wouldn't believe. Imagine a creature that has in its hereditary traits the ability to live forever."

"You collect their skulls too?" Wanting to disagree, I look away.

"Imagine taking in that trait." Khristoff reaches into the engine's opening and removes a foul-smelling clump of mulch.

Disgusted, I cover my nose and mouth. The smell of churning fat and fur fills the tiny space with an odd memory. I remember visiting the caves with Sherianne, we had the time of our lives watching the bats fly from their rocky perch to their jousting partners. I never figured the bats were attacking each other for survival. Khristoff flicks the mass of mulch onto the ground, slapping the panel closed.

The lights from the ceiling bounce off Khristoff's Silver Collar. While I am aware of my citizen's duty to report this interaction, my lack of responsibility is ingrained in the situation as I unconsciously stare at the Collar around his blackened neuro-metal neck.

"Have you ever bartered for your innocence?" Khristoff approaches, holding the screwdriver in his bloody hand.

"What are you talking about?" I wake from the thoughts in my head, trying not to think of the smell.

"Imagine a world without the need to purchase everything." He focuses on my body language. "Imagine life without the urge to follow." He looks up at the ceiling, staring at an obscured point in the sky. "Imagine connecting everyone in a realm most comfortable, where the impression of heaven is closer than we all think."

I picture in my mind a great pyramid. Believed to be the first man-made structure, the pyramids of Egypt were staples in humanity's interpretation of the very beginning. Even as wonders that glorified the afterlife, the pyramids were not built to survive the storms of the apocalypse. I imagine the city of Thicket as one of the great pyramids and as a wonder that shaped the making of the modern world. I feel I may contrast my fellow citizens' beliefs with those of ancient Egypt, having to hear the electronic voice of the new world's self-proclaimed savior.

"You can't read people's minds," I feel lost. "Or access their faith."

"I'm curious --"

Khristoff tilts his head, stabbing the top of my thigh with the screwdriver.

I scream in agony as a feeling of hopelessness fills my lungs. My body falls limp as he digs the screwdriver deeper into my leg muscle.

"Imagine --" he slowly twists the screwdriver, creating a tearing sensation to the echo in my voice. "--knowing God exists." He twists in the opposite direction. "In the heart of every person in Thicket."

"Stop," I speak softly, staring at the blood that is pooling under me.

"I can't hear you." He pulls the screwdriver out of my thigh.

"What do you want?" I try to apply enough pressure to stop the bleeding.

"You will bring me the cube." He moves my hands away, allowing my blood flow to resume.

"The what?" I feel confused, hoping for a miracle.

"You're smart, Sunder," he stretches his hand over the open wound and a warm light envelopes my leg. "But I own you."

In an instant, Khristoff's palm cauterizes my wound. Although the pain remains, I can see that the bleeding has stopped.

"If you want to see your daughter again, you'll bring me the comp-ucube."

"What?" I glance back at the entry-port as it emits the sounds of turning gears. "How do you know about the cube?"

The entry-port opens in a loud transition and Shantelle appears in a small cloud of dust that quickly settles. The corners of her mouth have an accumulation of saliva that resembles ivory foam and dark rings have now appeared around her eyes. I watch her move from the entry-port as I try to massage the pain from my leg.

"You have 4 hours." Khristoff motions for Shantelle to sit.
"What?" I want to know more. "I can barely walk."

Khristoff speaks to me but watches Shantelle walk across the room to the compression engine. He smiles as she tries to operate her comp-uzync while using the engine as a bench.

Khristoff's gaze seems to shatter. "Your daughter is more than broken. She may not be as lucky." His eyes brighten as if more electricity is passing through a nuclear outlet.

I do my best to stand without falling to my knees. Looking toward the large panels of the wasteland entry-port, I feel powerless in believing I would be able to make the journey back to the city.

Khristoff hovers over Shantelle as she fails to properly operate her comp-uzync. He lowers a forefinger to her device and a tiny jolt of electricity jumps across an inch of recycled air, restarting her comp-uzync into working order again. "Jessica is just another creature in my possession. She wanted a home.

She wanted to be something more."

"And now? Why should I believe you?" I grab my leg, unable to deny his strength.

Ignoring my question, Khristoff uses his comp-uzync to access the suite's supply shuttle. Like a miner's dolly, hauling drilling equipment miles through the earth's crust, the suite's shuttle can transport two prone passengers across the miles of rocky terrain.

"Sunder," Khristoff starts, petting Shantelle's dirty orange hair. "You think you have a choice. I dare you to fake your courage." The electricity in his eyes flicker to the sounds in his voice, illuminating the hood covering his face.

I mumble as I step through the entry-port, having to kneel to board the tiny transport. Feeling the rough condition of its passenger seat and watching the round glass dome flip and latch into place gives me the thrill as if this trip is part of someone else's day.

Today is turning into the worst. I find that the worst in any situation is to be expected, while still assuming situations like this would never happen to me. I fantasize about curling into my bed and going back to the way things were yesterday.

The thought of searching Thicket makes me feel like an innocent child lost in a maze of grown-up ideas. A small part of me still accepts the power of belief but an alarming portion of my career has led me further from the truth.

Sometimes I think that the Silver Collar Society is to blame for everything wrong in the world. Having abandoned my faith for the sake of SCS showcases a personal connection to the desert. Khristoff sounds as if he wants to make things right.

Khristoff wants me to believe that the absconder's mentality and way of life is complete. There may be no other way to truly live. Like another loyal pet ordered by a simple command, I see no use in struggling. He has my daughter's life at his disposal and there is nothing I can do short of listening to what he wants. I simply count each passing mountain on my solitary journey back to the city, thinking of Jessica, remembering Sherianne, and thanking God for this opportunity to regain a part of me that could have been lost forever.

Chapter 9

Heartbeat of God

..

"And there you shall remember your ways and all your
deeds with which you have defiled yourselves, and you
shall loathe yourselves for all the evils that you have
committed."

Ezekiel 20:43

..

The most I can remember about Jessica comes
through what I can recall about Sherianne. As an infant
remains hidden in the warm folds of its parent's arms,
my opaque memories of Jessica and her mother come
back to me in scattered details of their absconder
encampment. The sun shines over the barren
landscape, highlighting areas of dead earth where I
once traveled.

As my solo trip on the suite's shuttle takes in the
view of the approaching landscape, I am reminded of
the way Sherianne used to move in the morning. She
would dress for the marketplace in her best attire, and I
would watch as I always enjoyed. She would eat her
daily pieces of nutrient-rich cauliflower with a smile
while I did the same. I envisioned a perfect life
together, free from worry and doubt that anything
dramatic would change our future.

With the passing of each low-lying hill and jagged
mountain range, I think back to my younger years
when daily life involved less stress. Longing for
another carefree chapter in my life, I remember the

149

love that found me a wife.

I met Sherianne when I was a teenager, at an age when a few big decisions were soon to change my life. Around that time, I hoped for someone to take me away from this mundane world. On a SCS guided tour around the outskirts of the city, I saw an exciting employment opportunity as well as the future love of my life in the guise of a young, rustic-blonde naturalist. The color scheme in Sherianne's hair seemed unnaturally beautiful even as it appeared the brightest in direct sunlight. I would never forget the wave in her long curls or the way she tucked a single strand behind her ears when she had something important to say. To me, she seemed more perfect than any citizen in Thicket, which did not sit well with my parents.

As I witness the mountain ranges of Hetch Hetchy Valley clustering together, I remember my parents and the stern look of disappointment on my mother's face. From the time of my licensed birth, I was raised by a couple who followed every rule enforced by the Silver Collar Society. The city's population limit had been regulated from the first years of breaking ground, anticipating a heavy fluctuation in elders who wish to preserve their family bloodline.

I never had a brother or sister because of the policy against siblings. The people of Thicket were forced to curb their breeding urges while those who chose to rebel against the system multiplied based on sexual occurrences. I never experienced the joys and sorrows of sharing my genes with another person until the day I

150

met my daughter, Jessica.

Like all legitimate children in Thicket, I attended a school operated by SCS officials. In addition to people from the community, I learned from specialists who helped me develop the skills necessary to better serve my city.

It took me years to understand that the educational system was organized to flush out the early signs of a natural born genius, and those children who were deemed this highest honor became the property and responsibility of the Silver Collar Society.

I was one who SCS considered a gifted child, which meant extensive education and research in the development of neuro-applications, adding to a tiny fragment of arrogance that remained with me throughout my teenage years. I do not want to believe the woman Jessica has grown up to be. Being a product of an illegal union, Jessica would have had to live outside the city and endure the skills of an absconder.

As the shuttle starts to slow on its path to the city, my vessel approaches the outer entry-port, which opens and then closes behind me. Inside a segment of the city's infrastructure, I am reminded of the way Sherianne held baby Jessica in her arms, how she would stop crying the instant she saw her mother's beautiful face.

My motionless stare is interrupted by the loud opening of the inner entry-port, throwing around the contents of my stomach with the momentum of a breaking vehicle. Somewhat dazed, as if returning from a trip back in time, the glass door flips open, and I succumb to the returning smells of the southwest corner of the marketplace. Before taking my first step back onto the neuro-metal pavement, my stomach turns. I feel nervous.

The sounds of the busy cityscape quickly fill the tiny shuttle as I struggle to stand. People nearby focus on me with stares of confusion and gawks of jealousy, having never seen this shuttle system used before. A surprise to the hundreds nearby when I step out, and do not claim to be from a different world where life is better than it currently is. How sad that no one thought of this until it was too late.

I move away from the sealing shuttle as nearby pedestrians close to me surround the transport, not wanting to board but shamelessly displaying their curiosity. Among the chattering bystanders eager to get a hands-on-look, I hear the mention of Uni's name and the chances of his crazy stories being true. Not surprised, I venture out, away from the crowd, thinking about Uni's odd habits and the presses I sell, wondering if they really are vermin-free.

A large portion of the marketplace has grown weary of Uni's slanderous rumors, but rarely do they act with authoritative discipline. The more Uni speaks of the Silver Collar Society and the vermin used to feed the population of Thicket, the less the people listen. Most people ignore Uni as they pass him on the streets. When he speaks of Khristoff and the legend of the immortal man, people gather to ponder his accurate findings. Like the early critics to a conspiracy theory, questions lead to Uni ranting. It runs a vicious cycle.

Thinking of the comp-ucube, I recall a younger man who helped distract SCS when Sherianne and Jessica escaped the city. A debt worth the lives of my family is forever tied to a device I consider too important to be used against the public's will.

Walking through the city takes longer now that I am in pain, maneuvering through crowds that seem to be venturing in the opposite direction. I roll up the sleeves of my desert suit, which slip down with the brushing of more people. I then raise my elbows to push a way through the men and women who glance back with concerns of their personal space.

Rather than get involved with a random person over an elbow raised or a shoulder scrapped, I mind my own business. As the streets divide me from the crowds, I notice people seem to be gathering on the other end of the marketplace, while only a handful linger near the steps of the cathedral.

What I remember best about entering a place of worship was my courtship with Sherianne before I had any permanent deal with SCS. She had been eager to speak with a priest, who at the time was a spontaneous young man named Miko. The cathedral was built to be a booming capital where people of various faiths could come to congregate under a single roof. When Sherianne entered the elaborate building with me at her side, the cathedral was filled with hundreds of people silently praying to their own deities.

153

Dozens of priests in black robes roamed the outer walkways of the cathedral. They each wore a Silver Collar as if it represented a symbol of authority over penance. A priest of Thicket could absolve the sins of several religions without the need of a translator. Today, less than half a dozen priests roam the church halls.

The tall staircase to the cathedral invites every citizen to count the steps on their way into the great hall. Each step is engraved in ascending roman numerals. Those who choose to loiter in front of the building each day usually occupy specific steps that remind them of the number of their sins in hopes of being forgiven. An old woman at the top step hugs her knees, mumbling about a little boy she was not able to save.

The archway to the cathedral is over four meters high, adapted to host more than a single deity. The six reseeded steel blades, safely hidden below me, are still capable of slicing me in half. As two Nephilim-sized statues of the human condition tower over me, I feel my sense of self-confidence dwindle in the male's physique, slowing my pace across the quiet aisles of the main hall.

Sitting on opposite sides of the vast building, two priests with Silver Collars focus on the same mural of reassembled glass that decorates the back of the hall. My eyes dart between the two Silver Collars that sparkle in the sun's filtered light.

The emptiness of the main hall keeps me in silence as I take a seat in the pew directly behind one of the priests. Unwilling to hesitate on Jessica's behalf, I lean forward as if I am kneeling in prayer. I lose myself in my leg's pain with my hands pressed together, wondering what is so incredibly important about having control over the cube. Does Khristoff want a revolution against the only system large enough to prove a successful method of perseverance? Does he want the same thing?

I start to wonder if the city's entire population is really at stake. The advanced nature of the neuro-metal technology has continued to spark my interest from the first schematic I designed to the creature living as Father Khristoff. Absconders are vengeful and extremely territorial. If not for the public displacement of a young boy who knew the end was near, a wasteland rebellion would never have been formed.

I close my eyes in disappointment, feeling horrible for the child torn from his family and friends over a piece of scribbled poetry. I feel sorry for the teenager who had to survive the desert by joining those who wanted nothing to do with the city's way of life. I cast my attention on the mural in front of me and I feel sympathetic for the young adult who could no longer live a normal life, bonding with a material that would forever change his DNA. More than an injection into the bone marrow, Khristoff smeared his wounds in neuro-metal. I would rather not test his strength in negotiation, so I cannot sit back and let my daughter be harmed.

When I think back to the hunched creature holding a handful of mulched vermin, I realize he has complete control over the city's water supply. If something were to prevent his satisfaction, he could contaminate the population. The frustration and disgust leave me feeling obligated to respect the work of art that Loy has created.

The longer I choose to dwell on Khristoff's state of madness, the more I feel like acting out irrationally, hoping all the disharmonious events I have recently experienced will snap back into a proper reality. Even as my leg aches and my hips twitch in this position of penance, I sense a greater power that keeps me kneeling in place. The sight of two motionless Silver Collars, reflected in a green sparkle, assures me that nothing has changed. Are these feelings about lost hope and regretful opportunities all in my head?

The silence in the cathedral quickly dissolves across the rippling sounds of heavy footsteps approaching from behind. As a last resort I feel I could jump over the pew in front of me and use the priest as a disorientated obstacle. The Collars who feel compelled to have me run would find me soon enough and eventually there would be no place left in the city to hide. With each slow step that I hear shuffle in the large hall, I shift part of my weight in anticipation of running.

I glance back and see the reflection of a Silver Collar who seems to be wandering in my direction. The black robe that cloaks the figure reminds me of Khristoff, except for a circular insignia that highlights his chest. The religious logo is a combination of every belief, collaborating into a hybrid design, illustrating the fact that all religions eventually come together as one. As the robed figure sits in the pew behind me, he speaks in a raspy tone that seems to drag through my memory like a lead anchor.

"Less and less show each day." The priest folds his hands into his lap, retaining his focus on the mural. "I remember when this hall filled every morning and sunset. I remember a time when there wasn't room for everyone to sit."

I lean back, standing from my position of penance and sitting in the pew. The priest's ideals seem strangely familiar, as if I have heard them somewhere before. A sure assumption shakes me into a widened stare at the old friend sitting behind me.

"All this time?" I look back, surprised.
"Taken seriously." Miko sounds sincere in his gentle voice.
"Do you still protect the young?" I break the tension in bridging our pasts. "I remember when you carried the tiniest of living dreams with the biggest of smiles." I smile as I recall the image of Miko holding baby Jessica moments after Sherianne gave birth.

Miko's distant stare springs into my field of vision as if he has heard a bogus rumor. Although my smile is more pronounced and the first feature Miko recognizes, the priest sounds confused.

"Sunder?" He points to the top of my head. "What

happened to the mane?"

"Well, I would call it stress." I rub the baldness of my scalp, combing over the front of my receding hairline.

I believe in the manifestation of my past, controlling my current state, and feel strong in my hair loss being associated with the raids on Sherianne's camp. I know that working against the Silver Collar Society is responsible for my lack of charismatic appeal.

"What happened here?" I turn in my seat, placing my arm on the back of the pew.

"Don't you remember?" Miko looks on to the reassembled glass that depicts the four catastrophic events leading to the city's creation and the power and authority of the Silver Collar Society.

I remember when floods conjoined into continental tsunamis, earthquakes grounded more than violent aftershocks, volcanoes generously advertised toxic explosions, and worldwide famine influenced the illusive disease that continues to eat away the outer wastelands and its remaining inhabitants. By the end of the late 2050's, the worst of the natural disasters had peaked, and by witness to the earth's steady demise, the Silver Collar Society stepped in to propose a solution that would save the last of humanity.

The city of Thicket was constructed to be mankind's last wish for peace. By the beginning of the 2100's, mankind had advanced its neuron-technology while it rapidly retracted any need for ecological support. The surrounding land outside the strongest city on earth had become barren, a wasteland where humans once decided to let the forests burn, the animals die, and the lakes dry up.

Those in the privately funded scientific fields, such as electrical and biological engineering, found an alternative way to sustain a city of tomorrow's only hope. For the price of their own neurosis to live, humans sacrificed all that did not maintain their postmodern cause.

Miko clears his throat. "We lost our ozone layer but gained a new level of protection. We may live on a dead planet, but we can resurrect ourselves."

The city of Thicket was erected in a nine-year time span, battling against six months of extreme heat and six months of extreme cold each year. Spanning the surface of the Hetch Hetchy Valley, the city of reseeded steel created a new home for the last of the human population in the summer of 2061. Construction workers from several neighboring states worked around the clock to lay the foundation for the largest project in earth's history.

"Neuro-metal was introduced as a life-preserving material." Miko scratches the tar like surface that covers a large portion of his left forearm. "It can carry an electrical current and be manipulated with a control chip, adhering to any surface to form the strongest conduction in existence."

"Listen to you now," I hold up a finger and trace the number one in the air. "You get a bonus point."

"Millions of gallons of neuro-metal, Sunder. Nonstop production was needed to create this city, so of course it led to an all-out rebellion." Miko looks back at the glass murals of catastrophic events. The third mural depicts the rise of the human right's movement, boycotting the use of neuro-metal research alongside the publicly supported need for more desert suits. "Those who opposed its use and anything that had to do with SCS were forced to wander. Those who remained in the desert, transformed their way of life."

A majority of the population in Thicket knows of the absconder race and the intimidating lives they lead. Most absconders simply smell bad, but in large numbers, every single one is to be feared. Throughout the 2080's, the rise of absconders led to control of city streets and the revolt of half the population. Turning the city into a giant pornographic waterfall of showcases, absconders quickly gained the support of everyone not comfortable with the debt claimed by elites of the Silver Collar Society.

"Fortunately for our children, SCS felt like they had enough of the revolt and introduced the first Collar to patrol the streets, taking the law into their own hands." Miko pushes a dozen buttons on his comp-uzync, illuminating a holographic display of a news article from a day in history that blocks the glass murals from view. "Imagine life without the urge to follow. Four years after the Collars were introduced, the last of the absconders were driven out of the city."

The holographic news article reads, ALL ABSCONDERS REMOVED FROM THICKET. I remember my parents showing me this same article soon after my seventh birthday, conditioning me to be grateful for a world free of absconder domination. Until my daughter's birth in 2203, I had to keep my life separate from those who tried to live outside the city. I look up at the news article that slowly flickers out of existence, leaving my glare fixed upon the glass mural.

"It's all because of SCS that I couldn't raise my own child. Jessica couldn't stay with me. Sherianne couldn't stay with her parents. No one could know about Jessica. Her birth had to be kept a secret. I wish I could have taken them back with me, but I had to leave them behind." My words break on the verge of showing emotion.

"You did the right thing, Sunder." Miko leans forward and places a hand on my shoulder. "If SCS knew about your involvement with either one of them, things could have been worse."

I cannot help but think that the hypothetical situation Miko ponders is already happening. Perhaps the Silver Collar Society knew about my involvement with Sherianne's camp and that was why Crowchest was raided. They could have found out about Jessica and now think that she is responsible for everything.

I am reminded of the way Sherianne looked up at the stars, the way she smiled while waiting for the upcoming meteor shower to occur. We would sit in silence and stare into the heavens, counting the stationary lights as precursors to the ultimate show. Sherianne would curl her head into my shoulder when the meteors started to fall, whispering small promises

161

for the next year of our lives together.

"Miko, I need to get her back." I look up with tears on my cheeks. "I have no idea what happened to Sherianne. I have to at least make sure Jessica is safe."

"Sunder, do you remember the day you left the wastelands, and returned to the city without your family?"

"I think about it all the time." It hurts to admit such a flaw in my past.

"Have you asked God to watch over them? Have you prayed for God to protect them?"

"I thought I didn't have to. I figured Sherianne was strong enough for both of them."

"You can't place your faith in man, Sunder. Even if it's your own wife." He lays a hand on the back of the pew. "You must put some of your faith in the Lord. Only he can make sure that they will be fine."

"Can he guarantee they get enough to eat? Can he insure they have a shelter to protect their heads? What can he promise? Safe passage into Heaven? Be like SCS and promise an eternity of peace for the price of loyalty? I can't think of the end of the road for them. Not yet anyway." I shake my head, failing to admit the arrogance in my voice.

"You can't do this to yourself."

"It's not on purpose." I keep my face hidden.

"You can't keep blaming yourself for the life they needed to live. God chose a way for them to survive. And he did the same for you."

"He doesn't have a plan for everyone." I hold my arms out. "I mean, look at this place. Is it by coincidence that these people are the last strands of human DNA?"

"God has a story of purpose for you, Oscar. If your gift is to fix the system, do so, and do it with a hopeful heart. Do it enthusiastically. Your purpose is clear."

"My path may be clear, but Jessica doesn't have that luxury."

"Where is she now?"

"I don't know. I haven't --" I wipe the tears from my eyes and clear my throat, hoping to bring back the masculine tone in my voice. "-- haven't seen her yet."

"Do you think she's hurt?"

"I don't know. That thing's holding her." I curl my lip, thinking of Khristoff's bent form.

"The immortal man." As if he agrees, Miko sits back in his seat and looks forward. "Do you know the tale of the man who tried to live forever? There are a million excuses for immortality, but Khristoff seems to be the one who could produce the only reason."

"There's no reason for what he wants." I ponder Khristoff's rational thought to harboring a powerful device.

"Then why would an absconder want such a device?" Miko asks casually.

"You tell me." I stand from my seat, hoping he knows that secrets should remain silent.

Miko looks surprised, as if caught in a lie.

"He said the future of Thicket was at stake." I move away from the pew and linger in the main aisle. "He shouldn't even know it exists."

"Sunder, I understand that your daughter means the world to you, but do you realize what you are saying?" His focus remains fixed on my stressful pace.

"I know you believe in this whole thing," I look

163

around the cathedral. "But how can you make spiritual claims with a prototype?"

"Imagine a creature that has in its hereditary traits the ability to live forever. People like Khristoff don't give back their prized possessions. They fight for their trophies and will kill to retain it."

"I realize that, but now he thinks I can provide a direct link to God."

"Is he wrong?" Miko lifts an eyebrow, creating an awkward moment of silence.

"Why though?" I start.

"I don't know. I've had several teenagers try to steal it, and each time they got a little bit closer."

Miko looks at the back of the cathedral as he stands from the pew and moves toward the center wall. His robe drags along the floor as we both climb the staircase to the upper balcony and reseeded steel altar. Hidden from my view, his fingers caress the sides of the altar, feeling for a compartment switch that opens the top portion of the altar. Slowly, a submerged level appears with the comp-ucube.

Coined in my scientific discovery, the comp-ucube's design originated through the hard connection of two comp-uzyncs, linking the similar systems into a single processor capable of expanding its own storage components. Later redesigned as a single unit without the need of a display screen, input dial pad, or power host, the comp-ucube became the shell casing for a new type of neuro-metal appendage.

Miko lifts the cube from the altar and holds it out for me to see. "Sunder, tell me what you see."

Wondering if the priest's question has some significant value, I answer with a slanted expression. "A cube?"

"What else?" he descends the staircase slowly, inviting me to walk with him.

"Alright. I see, a single outcome." My gaze with the cube remains unbroken as I step in unison with my old mentor. "It gives off the illusion of control."

"But we have the control." Miko holds the cube outward, threatening to drop it down the remaining stairs.

"You call this control?" I raise my comp-uzync, shaking it between us. "This is just another form of luxury."

"Yes," he lifts the cube to his eye level. "To better mankind may be the only luxury we can afford. Imagine a world without the need to purchase everything. When I look at the cube, do you know what I see?"

"An interlude to your sermon?"

"The heartbeat of God," bringing the comp-ucube to his chest.

"Heartbeat?" My eyebrows lift in amazement as I smile under my view. "I guess I'm limited in my social constructs." I look out over the empty cathedral as we near the halfway point. "I wouldn't have guessed religious control."

"A sight like you wouldn't believe."

Having conducted experiments with the prototype that would ultimately help me design the final device, the comp-ucube was originally engineered to diagnose overall human health. The neuro-metal casing is no different than the city's walking pavement, reminding me of ribbons of hardened sludge. The electrical current that runs through the streets of Thicket is the same source of energy that emanates from the comp-ucube.

"Or a conspiracy theory," counting the number of empty pews.

"Nothing of the sort," Miko scoffs. "And abandon the truth?"

"Obviously," I roll my eyes.

"You would destroy it?"

"I don't know." I rub the pain in my leg, feeling each step. "I thought I had a plan."

"And how far have you strayed?"

I think about the memories of Sherianne, the schematics of the comp-ucube, and the rest of my life contained on the Imprint Drive that was stolen from me. Remembering my intention to build a better world, I try to justify the option of returning to bad habits. I wanted the comp-ucube to link together those with an implant, but never followed through with what that meant to my promise.

"I wanted to help bring people together."

"Is that why you dumped it here?" Miko holds the prototype comp-ucube close as he reaches the ground level of the staircase, refusing to walk any further.

"I wanted to be safe."

"And?"

"And now, I'm not sure."

As if accepting my deflated response, Miko turns and looks up at the glass display, slowly lowering his eyelids. He lets out a soft sigh while still clutching the comp-cube close to his heart.

"It means that much?" I see him containing his smile.

"And you? What do you believe?" Miko opens his eyes, eager to hang on every word.

"I believe I can get my daughter back." My words come across as if desperate in needing to prove a point. "I believe I can save her life."

"Sunder, don't confuse bloated belief with faith." He glances at my comp-uzync. "You can't barter with him."

"I can't?" I cross my arms, glancing at the comp-ucube. "Not unless I have something he wants."

"When you first brought it here, you said people were trying to steal it from you. Now you want to give it away."

The thought of betrayal keeps me silent. The anxiety of breaking my promise sets in my stomach, twisting me of all responsibility.

"Barter for your innocence, Sunder," Miko snaps as he turns away, clutching the device like stress-relief toy. "Some people are born with a gift. Others, a purpose. Whether you lead or follow, everyone contributes. You need the cube. I need an heir."

"A what?"

"You bring Shantelle back with the cube, and we have a deal." He turns back, holding out his hand to offer a shake.

"Why her?"

"Youth has its advantages," he jokes. "But the

167

answer is in her DNA. Imagine connecting everyone in a realm most comfortable, where the impression of heaven is closer than we all think." Again, he offers his free hand. "Do we have an agreement?"

I think back on the years I wasted not fighting for my family. The moments I lost to the requirements of my job. The life I could have enjoyed is so far in the past that it may be impossible to recognize, even with digital memories. I pull out the drawing of Sherianne and I start to feel happy again, as if the life I had is close enough to touch.

Hesitant to shake hands for such a deal, I measure the thought of saving my daughter's life, wondering if it outweighs the life of a teenage scavenger who could have died in that cave. Tucking the drawing back into my suit, I stretch out my hand and Miko pulls me close. Our shaking hands send ripples through his robe, and I can feel our deal closing as if I am forced to watch from an outside perspective. He whispers into my ear.

"Imagine knowing God exists in the heart of every person. We may find out in our lifetime." He pauses to look into my eyes. "A savior among us."

I feel a chill running up my spine, caressing my skin like the pins and needles of another bad habit. The smile in Miko's expression reminds me of Arlita and the spiritual belief she guards so well. She trusts her faith with such fortitude that she would never approve this transaction. I can hear her voice of reason in my head, where my consciousness should be guiding me.

With her words of scripture returning to my memory, I now understand what Arlita meant. Why the priests of SCS oppose outside control. It seems as if I have no say in the matter when making this deal. I feel pinned against an imperialist, with nothing else to give.

When our hands separate, I am holding the comp-ucube and Miko is crossing the hall, acting as if our conversation had not taken place at all. With each step toward the cathedral's open entryway, I feel the bubbles of guilt floating to the surface of my soul. The cold stare of the female statue seems more appropriate the second time around.

Outside the cathedral, I quickly feel like I made a mistake. I realize that I have conducted a compromise with a man of God to deliver an unknowing person for the chance to save another. Is this deal fair? Is it my decision to bargain the life of one young girl for the other? As I descend the large stone steps of the cathedral, the heavy blades of the entry-port slowly move upward, as if closing behind me in solace for the mistakes I will continue to make.

The old woman sitting at the top step is still hugging her knees. She mumbles to herself, blaming her life for the loss of another. Will this be my future? With the comp-ucube in my hand, I walk by the old woman, surprising her as I brush her shoulder. She pulls back in fear, losing her balance, she starts to tumble down the stairs.

"Easy --" I quickly grab her shoulder and pull her

back onto her stoop, which seems to calm her hectic rocking. "Don't make things worse."

The old woman reaches up and holds onto my hand, locking eyes with someone who has taken the time to notice her. "You know my son. You know him --"

She starts crying in her apologies, begging for someone to heed her advice. "You know him, my son. Follow the willow. Follow the tracks. He isn't bad. He's all thumbs. All thumbs --"

The old woman repeats the same line as if she needs to convince the demons of her past to move on. I take a step back, which does not seem to halter her rants. Tucking the comp-ucube into the folds of my desert suit, I continue down the stone steps of the cathedral.

The few people who linger along various steps look up and lock eyes with me as I pass them, sympathizing with my attempt at comforting a deranged woman. Near the bottom of the steps, a young girl trips at my feet. I instantly recognize her from the East Sector Club.

"Sunny!" Laci pauses, hoping to catch her breath. "You've got to help!"
"Hold up. What's going on?" I reach out to help keep her standing.
"It's Thumbs! Uni is going to kill Thumbs!"

Chapter 10

Burnt Offerings

..

"And your offspring shall possess the gate of his enemies, and in your offspring, shall all the nations of the earth be blessed, because you have obeyed my voice."

Genesis 22:18

..

Harsh winds battle against the Suite Oasis. Hail stones with a thunderous boom vibrate the reinforced roof. The changing hue of the horizon awakens Khristoff's imagination as he pets Shantelle's dirty hair. Alone with his daughter, he orders her awake.

"Get up, the sun is falling."
"So?"
"So, we're like the Mesoamericans and the Persians. We're like the Greeks and the Egyptians. I'm like Abraham and you're my unfortunate son. We have a schedule."

Tired and unconvinced, Shantelle slouches in her movement. Khristoff approaches the heavy entry-port to the wastelands, pulling on a large lever. The circular entry-port rotates open and a wave of hot desert air crashes into the open workstation of the Oasis.

The wasteland sunsets are an encouraging sight. Playing off the jagged terrain of South Tahoe's dry lakebed, venomous Hyltots awaken and begin to scurry. Khristoff pushes Shantelle through the entry-port to feel the difference a sunset makes.

The evening air smells just as putrid as the afternoon swelter, but the severe heat is no longer a problem. Shantelle watches the dispersing clouds, feeling her stomach digesting itself. She walks ahead a few yards and spots a solitary Hyltot.

"There's one!" She points.

Another heavily armored Hyltot flickers between Shantelle's legs. Determined to prove herself, she changes direction and takes several long steps to follow the brave lizard, cornering it against a broken boulder and discharged canister. Khristoff approaches from behind and grabs the frightened creature.

"Can I name it?" She watches it cower in her father's grip.

Khristoff watches Shantelle melt over the Hyltot's leathery beak, sharp claws, and scaly tail. He glares at her infatuation over a creature that, if threatened, could kill her. In a moment of rage, Khristoff marches back into the Suite.

"Wait! What are you doing?" She tries to stop him from walking away with her new pet.

Khristoff tightens his grip around the Hyltot's neck. Its eyes close and blood, easily mistaken for mercury, begins to seep from its lids. The lizard's small head separates from its body and falls to the floor, bouncing off Khristoff's knee and rolling away. He raises the headless Hyltot over a collection bin and squeezes, draining its venom and blood.

Between bursts of hysterical tears, Shantelle woefully inspects the collection bin and a splash of Hyltot blood catches her in the face. She falls back, foolishly smearing the acidic silver liquid across her lips.

"It's in my mouth!"

Khristoff throws the bloody Hyltot into the bin and grabs Shantelle's face, "And your time's up."

With an intense glow, Khristoff absorbs the Hyltot's blood, cauterizing the burn scars across Shantelle's face. Crippled by the Hyltot toxin, Shantelle drops to her knees, buckling by the immense pain in her throat. Paralysis forms and her vision fades into darkness.

Chapter 11

Case of Paralysis

..

"The one who conquers and who keeps my works until the end, to him I will give authority over the nations."

Revelation 2:26

..

Business in the West Sector Marketplace can be successful. As deeply religious citizens shop the streets surrounding the Cathedral in lieu of a luxurious salvation, I try to ignore anyone begging for a second chance. I cannot ignore the alarm of a hysterical young girl.

"It's Thumbs! Uni is going to kill Thumbs!"

"You're joking, right?" I curl an eyebrow, reflecting on the soft nature of the babbling salesman I passed earlier.

"I'm serious!" Laci pushes me, disheveling my desert suit. "You have to hurry," she grabs me by the wrist and leads me away from the cathedral. The more she pulls my arm, the faster I trip over my feet.

While being pulled against my will, I follow with a frown, thinking if not for my inherent disfavor of running, I would not have been involved. I could have dodged Anneli's presence at my apartment entryway, making the quick step around her to a quiet room inside and I wouldn't have to return to Khristoff needing to save another disrespectful youth.

Laci pulls on my arm, leading me through crowds

of bystanders who are oblivious to the commotion she can vaguely describe. She leads me through occupied alleyways and under link-rail tubes that continue to commute people who know nothing of our endeavor. Soon, she is leading me through herds of people who speak of a spectacle in the marketplace. I overhear people speaking in various languages as we pass them.

"The girl's dead!" A woman rants in French.

"They'll take him away after this, I'm sure of it," her husband confesses.

I want to interject, but perhaps they know more about the situation than I have witnessed. Uni would never be a physical threat to anyone, this has to be a big misunderstanding. As I think of how to defend an old friend, we arrive to see Uni with his bloody hands around the neck of a young boy, and I cannot deny the people around him.

"Back off! This is for his own good!" Uni yells at an encroaching man.

"Let the boy go!" An elderly woman exclaims.

"No one can let it go!" Uni licks the air over his right shoulder, tasting his invisible salt block. "He's destroying our way of life!"

"Uni!" I try to flag his attention. "It's Oscar, remember?" I take a step closer to the struggle. "Tell me what happened."

"She stole my presses!" Uni gestures to the unconscious body of Laci's older sister, Anneli, with a small puddle of blood around her head and Cau-li scattered at her feet. He flexes his grip around the boy's neck. "This one wants control!"

175

"Okay, Uni. How's he going to take control?" I raise a hand, pointing to the boy's throat. "He can barely breathe."

"He's turning us against each other!"

The open wound on Anneli's forehead triggers the maternal instinct in her surviving sibling. Laci rushes to hold Anneli's head and to wipe the blood from her face.

"A lot of people are against you right now." I draw close to the two siblings, wondering if they need any help.

"I won't be afraid!" Uni changes his grip, allowing Thumbs to breathe, but quickly tightens his mechanical fingers around the young boy's throat again.

"These people are going to hurt you, Uni." I point to the surrounding crowd. "I don't know what's going on, but I don't think they're going to let you go. Look at their faces. Look at the girl. They're saying you killed her."

"I didn't kill anybody!" Uni starts with tears forming.

"Murderer! You killed my sister!" Laci stands up.

The crowd around Uni grows tighter in an oppressive stance. Their whispers of justification are quickly silenced and replaced by suggestions of vengeance. Women with canes lift their walking aids above their heads. Men with crates ready them for an impact. Even those who are not willing to fight find an object nearby that can be used as a weapon. The rational ambiance of the marketplace is soon drowned out by the grinding and growling of teeth.

176

Uni's eyes are shaking as he sees the majority of those around him taking up weapons from ordinary items. What Uni once saw as a hydro-generator for sale is now a large block of metal with its crosshair on his own forehead. Fan blades that are for sale on the other side of the marketplace are now being distributed here at a double price for the sake of seeing Uni bleed. Trinkets of nearby vendors that Uni thought would never sell are now being sold quicker than they can be fabricated. Uni watches as those vendors around him sell through an entire day's inventory at the expense of seeing it used in his punishment.

"No more blame." Uni sounds as if he has finally caught his scapegoat. "No more revolution. No more death."

"No one wants to die, Uni." I reach out to persuade him. "Let the boy go. We can talk." I want to empathize but find my fake support to be disappointing.

"Tell them to back off. No clubs. No blades."

"I don't think they'll listen to me, Uni." I look over my shoulder at the approaching crowd that has turned into a mob, refusing to lower their weapons. "You have to release the boy."

"Get me out," he whispers to me.

Uni looks at the horizon of the mob and notices the reflection of someone wearing a Silver Collar. With tears gathered in the corner of his eyes, Uni licks the invisible salt block on his shoulder and releases his grip around Thumb's neck. As the boy falls to his knees, Laci runs up to catch him, pulling him away from Uni.

"We can't have you roaming our streets," a young man in the crowd wielding a reseeded steel bar speaks.

"The marketplace isn't safe anymore!" An elder woman exclaims in Italian.

I watch as Thumbs coughs to regain his breath. He looks at the angry mob and feels convinced in their rage against this sinister wrongdoing.

"This isn't over!" Thumbs rubs his throat as he addresses Uni, glaring at the crazy old man with intent to return with a weapon of his own.

"What are you all still standing around for?" I exchange glances of oppression with several citizens in the marketplace. "Did you forget about SCS?" I extend my forefinger in a wide radius, catching the faces of those with the closest reach. "You think they don't see you?"

"Murderer!" a voice surfaces from the mob but remains hidden from view.

"Who said that?" My stare darts from scalp to scalp, trying to catch the location of the familiar voice.

"A savior among us," a shorter man wearing a Silver Collar emerges from the middle of the mob. "With full authority."

"You know that's not procedure." I take a step to protect Uni from the approaching Collar.

Feeling proud of the mob, he snaps his fingers bringing two other Collars forward from nearby to pull me to the side. "You see, Oscar. Just because you don't

178

have the authority to cleanse evil, doesn't mean that others shouldn't be allowed to." He raises a hand to the mob who continues to hold various weapons above their heads, asking for their silence. "It all gets done."

"You don't have that right. You're not God." I try to wiggle free, but I can move no further than a single step.

"That's true, Sunder." He casually points to the sky, relating to my statement. "I'm not God."

For a second, I feel relieved. I start to feel like things may start to go my way. I imagine being released along with Uni to calibrate our priorities. I see this entire situation being dissolved and the crowd dispersed.

"But I do enjoy passing parts of him," he smiles. "One part I find therapeutic. Would you care to guess?"

"You vowed to be lenient," I recall the oath of a Silver Collar agent.

"Not really." He looks disappointed in my answer. "I vowed to fulfill justice."

Standing alone, Uni backs up against the wall, surrounded by his array of unsold merchandise and scattered Cau-li presses. He looks at the injured boy who stares back with eyes that are as much on fire as those in the crowd. Laci next to him, expresses the same look of hatred. Uni then looks to the Silver Collar agents who stand with reason to incite a civil war, unwilling to hold back the mob.

"Go home!" Uni starts with a crack in his voice.

"Leave me alone!" He pauses, wiping his bloody hands on his abdomen. "I'm no murderer! They're the ones!" He points to Thumbs and Laci, huddled over Anneli's body.

"Blather!" A voice in the crowd barks.

"Believe me!" Uni rebuttals.

"Liar!" Another voice exclaims.

"Please!" Uni defends.

The crowd sounds hysterical. Suddenly from the back of the gathering, a square object is launched in the air, becoming a projectile at the indicted salesman. The top-heavy block of reseeded steel slams into Uni's chest, causing him to fall to the pavement in a shower of sparks and blood while triggering others to throw their own deadly weapon.

A heavy rain of debris pummels his artificial body, denting his legs and twisting his arms, severing many of his original fingers and breaking his untreated collarbone. A large glass orb collides with Uni's forehead, fracturing his skull. His comp-uzync emits a loud buzz, an indication that his heart has stopped.

I hesitate, staring at Uni's tangled body at the edge of the marketplace, not wanting to advance. I simply fall to the ground where I'm standing and watch as blood escapes his body, soaking the fabric that was his vending platform. In the aftermath of this contribution, the Collars disappear into the crowd along with Thumbs and Laci. The sudden barrenness of the marketplace proves to me that no one wants to be seen as Thicket's populace in the aftermath of this brutality.

The emptiness in Uni's face brings me back to abandoning Sherianne. The same cruelty used in her containment is once again fresh, as I remember the bodies of women and children who had fallen in their escape from the rules of the Silver Collar Society.

In my vacant gaze over Uni's quiet, mangled body, I hear the voice of a containment crew reporting nearby. As I watch people treat his remains, I remain seated, remembering Sherianne and her closest friends among the casualties of the raid, their weather-burned hands pointing to their mistakes.

The contented crowd thins out while I sit trying to understand Uni's obsession. I reach for a piston from his mechanical hand while items in his collection are distributed to others in the marketplace. Abandoned projectiles that line the street from those who did not take part in his execution, like the presses that fell from Uni's stash box are left discarded, treated as poison.

My fondest memories of Uni are about our own government's control. Hysterical men always disclose the secrets that few understand. The city's supply of Cau-li is created with the remnants of vermin. A set of pink lips will always lead to the benign. Whatever Uni mumbled seems to be coming true, so why would he lie and blame Thumbs for Anneli's death?

As I slowly stand, leaving Uni's death in mourning, I notice the streets at the end of the marketplace are quieter. There is no longer a jabbering salesman to entice the last of the wandering crowd. There is no longer an interesting storyteller to scare children in their dreams. The friend I need is no longer able to cover my back during a time he's needed most. A part of me dies and tears form. I think about the strength Uni gave me and the fact that he would not want to see me cry, so I whisper a soft good-bye and walk away.

I make my way back to the entry-port that shuttled me to the city. The Suite Oasis is less than an hour away, but the distance on foot can take close to two days. I pass people on the street who acknowledge my bravery while clearing the path for those who would never befriend an enemy of the Silver Collar Society. Whoever I pass makes no difference in bringing back an old friend. When I reach the entry-port, I habitually lift my hand to a glass plate, hoping to engage the link-rail system.

Nothing happens.

I press several buttons, hoping to stumble over the correct sequence of coding, but again my access of entry is denied. When I pound my fist on the metal surface of the entry-port, the people in the area turn their heads. They may not know how to leave the city, but it is obvious to them that to operate this specific link-rail, I would need to possess the key.

Then I feel something. A vibration emanates from the lining of my desert suit. Thinking something must have been activated during the ordeal in the marketplace, I open my suit's inner pocket and notice the comp-ucube, purring on its own.

I hold the comp-ucube to the entry-port and the

purrs become louder, making me wonder if my device is capable of unlocking more. I place the comp-ucube against the surface of the entry-port's control panel and the purring turns into a growl. The comp-ucube overrides the controls and the entry-port opens with the link-rail pod ready for boarding.

"Sunny!" Laci sprints toward me from a crowd of marketplace patrons, pushing her way through.

I turn, lingering in the entry-port. "Are you okay? What's wrong?"

Laci approaches we with a warm embrace, sounding out of breath while discreetly passing an object into my suit pocket. She whispers in my ear.

"It's about Uni," she pulls away while keeping me close. "He didn't kill my sister."

"What?" My head straightens. "Then what the hell happened?"

"I've seen Thumbs lie for less."

"That's no excuse!" My agitated demeanor confuses my balance as I start walking back into the crowd. "Someone has to be held --"

"There's nothing you can do." She grabs my arm, holding me from returning to a storm. "Right now, anyways. His memories are too important to him."

Laci releases my arm, allowing me to reach my own conclusion. Unaware of my prior engagement, she makes a fist over her heart and moves it in a clockwise circle.

"I'm sorry about your sister." I touch her shoulder.

"You know," she starts while dodging my act of solidarity. "Father taught me about blame. To those who apologize first."

Without smiling, Laci exposes the back of her middle finger while walking away, a sharp example of how I imagine Jessica would have responded. I board the shuttle and the latching door clicks into place. In a matter of seconds, the transport is propelled in the direction of the Suite Oasis, leaving the city in the distance.

The shuttle ride is quiet. My mind starts to wander, but I can still feel the weight of the comp-ucube in the folds of my desert suit. As I stare out the window at the passing landscape of nearly impassible mountain terrains, the words of what I will say once reunited with my daughter bounce around my head. I think I will tell her that I love her. Assure her there is nothing left to fear and try to convince her there is room in the city for another citizen no matter where she grew up. I will hold her in my arms and never let her go. All my life, she slept silently. I've felt so confined all these years in a world so unfair. Trapped in her memory of a father who was never there for his family, I want to correct the faults I left in pieces.

I pray that I find her in peace. I pray that I find her well. I hope to God that she will be able to return with me and help reassemble the family I once protected.

As the transport slows in its approach, the outer entry-port opens and allows me to enter. The secondary entry-port opens as the first port seals, transferring me into a storage cradle for the Suite Oasis. The glass door flips open and as the sounds I make in struggling to stand rival the sounds from each ionizing filter, I do my best impression of an alarm.

"Khristoff!" I shout across the room.

A reply comes back in the form of a young girl's violent cough.

"I have the cube!" I walk through the open entry-port, looking around corners. "Show yourself!"

The mechanics room looks no different. A small compression engine still occupies the center of the room, surrounded by fragments of recycled steel. The collection bins connected by tubes to a massive filtration system are still producing drinkable water for every person in Thicket. The smell of fog has now filled the dark and slanted room.

"You're too late." Khristoff appears from behind a large pump that looks to be producing a darker-stained liquid. "Your daughter is gone."
"Where is she?" I take a step forward, feeling the pain in my leg, darting my eyes around the room.
Khristoff gestures to the pair of visible legs that stick out from behind a loud, overworked filter. "Suffering."

I move for the corner of the room but am halted by Khristoff's outreached hand. He slams me against a collection bin, grabs my leg and squeezes. The pain coursing through my thigh stiffens my hips and I jerk my lower back. I feel close to buckling at the knee and sinking to the ground.

"First, give me the cube." He glares at me with electricity in his eyes.

Unable to tear my eyes away from the visible legs that twitch with every cough, I quickly reach into my desert suit and retrieve the comp-ucube, pushing it into Khristoff's abdomen.

"Here! Now, let her go."

Khristoff squints as he looks down, seeming unwilling to believe my offer.

"Done." He releases his grip on my thigh, taking the comp-ucube from my hand.

As he holds the comp-ucube up to the light, forming a smile, the visible legs fold at the knees and the hidden figure emerges from behind the filter.

"Shantelle?" I look surprised but sound concerned. "Where's Jessica?"

Shantelle's hair is mated to her head as beads of sweat trickle down her jaw line. The accumulation of saliva has thickened at the corners of her mouth. She looks exhausted, barely able to support her own weight.

"You're really bad with faces, Sunder." Khristoff approaches Shantelle and wipes the foam from her mouth.

The image of Sherianne flashes in my head as I stand before the likeness of my beloved wife. I realize that I am staring at my own flesh and blood who deceived me from the very beginning. This is the same girl who defended her mother in the club like she was from the same last name. Shantelle found me in the marketplace, looking for a way to ruin my life, when in fact she came looking for a way to save her own.

"He doesn't want a daughter." Shantelle coughs and hangs her weight on Khristoff. "He's got his memories."

"You can't be my --" I look worried, refusing to accept the truth.

"-- Jessica?" Khristoff adds, allowing Shantelle to detach herself and take a step forward on her own. "She could be."

"You left her in that absconder camp." Shantelle slowly steps toward me. "You left her to die like the others."

"I didn't know the camp would be raided. I came back for you." My words sound as if I am speaking from the other corner of the room.

"Little late, don't you think? Seems like your kind of routine." Shantelle turns toward a bin filled with mulched vermin. "You can't save everyone, Sunny." She submerges her hands into the bloody collection of body parts.

My eyes blink in rapid accordance with every known traumatic event. I suddenly feel like I wasted the last sixteen years of my life.

"What more do you want from me?"

Khristoff's comp-uzync is triggered and a three-dimensional image of my family appears in the room.

I take a step back to compensate for the image resolution. "You knew about me --"

"I told Shantelle everything," Khristoff interrupts. "She came to me after losing her mother. She saw me as her father." The holographic image disappears and Khristoff's eyes brighten with an excess amount of electricity. "Ironic, isn't it?"

I glare at Khristoff and return my focus to Shantelle. "What's going on?"

Khristoff holds the comp-ucube close to his face, admiring the neuro-metal casing. A small jolt of electricity jumps from his forehead to the cube, waking the device into a low purr.

"All this for a fancy router?" I sound agitated. "What difference could you possibly make from out here?"

"I thought he'd be smarter." Shantelle smiles at Khristoff.

Khristoff places his hand on a working machine, feeling the hum and vibration like a second language.

"You have such a tiny window of reality, Sunder. Suppose I disable the heat shield. Would you be okay?"

Shantelle laughs, which turns into a cough. She

moves for the compression engine while Khristoff aides her in sitting.

"Nothing goes to waste." Khristoff smiles over Shantelle's hunched, frail body, petting the side of her face. "My father didn't believe in God."
"What are you talking about?"
"He said, man couldn't create such a powerful being." His eyes begin glowing brighter. "He told me, God created himself. Like God, no one says I was born. Like a circle, never will I die. I have grown alone in a place only I can call home. Until I can control eternity, I have no reason to exist."

Khristoff raises the comp-ucube in the air as a trophy for his ultimate plan.

"People will live on for generations. I will have favorites and they will grow with the warmth of their orange sun. I will watch them become capable of destruction and I will witness their dispute over my existence. They will grow to love me, but they will become distant and begin building walls of their own. They will twist and replace my existence with a new story. More will originate from this beginning. What you see as empty space is where heaven will exist."

Khristoff's manifesto reminds me of Miko and his attempt to uncover my faith. A collection of personal beliefs obtained without consent frightens me. If Khristoff believes that he now has the power to play God, the mass of the population is most certainly in danger. Innocent people need reassurance for honoring their faith.

"If you're so powerful, why didn't you get the cube yourself?"

Khristoff laughs in defense.

"Why send me all this way?"
"I enjoy watching you struggle," he smirks. "Who better to betray a man of the cloth than someone with a secret?"

My puzzlement keeps me rigid. My feeling of assurance in Miko's promise to look out for my family is quickly replaced by a feeling of betrayal. I picture the Silver Collar priest taking part in our conversation, completely aware of the innocent risks involved. I feel Miko was able to convince me to accept that this realm is no longer comfortable.

"Everyone has a secret." The comp-ucube's purr becomes louder.

Shantelle gestures from the center of the room, pointing to the device in Khristoff's hands.

"The tube goes into your comp-uzync."

Khristoff pulls the translucent nanotube from the corner of the comp-ucube's casing. Shantelle begins to cough again, now more violent than before. Her eyes roll into the back of her head as she falls off the compression engine, hemorrhaging into convulsions of her arms and legs. Even more saliva has accumulated in the corners of her mouth. I run to her side to hold her still.

"Poor thing." Khristoff speaks, ignoring her spasms. "Always playing." He inserts the translucent tube into his comp-uzync and, with a spark of electricity from his finger, he jump-starts the comp-ucube into a series of growls.

I hold Shantelle close to my chest, rubbing the sweat from her unconscious forehead. I can hear the growls from the comp-ucube getting louder as a kaleidoscope of colors illuminate the floating nanotube. The colors quickly blend together in a dark array, creating a visual example of hate.

"Yes!" Khristoff looks to the ceiling, absorbing the comp-ucube's power of information. "Memories! Millions of memories! I can see -- I can see everything!" He lifts the comp-ucube as he stutters. "I -- see -- God!"

A small stream of smoke escapes the side of the comp-ucube where the nanotube extends from its casing. Suddenly, a stream of smoke vents from the opposite side, clouding the local vicinity in an aroma of rancid decay.

"The end!" Khristoff's voice deepens, now carrying an electronic echo. "You are nothing without me!"

Khristoff approaches me, dragging his dark robe that seems to be disintegrating, falling apart in small segments. The smoke from the comp-ucube is now covering the ground. Springing from the cracks of

Khristoff's neuro-metal skin, the same rancid smoke douses his figure. The blackened color of his body begins to change in color, turning gray before transitioning to a red glow.

The temperature of Khristoff's body rises drastically, burning his internal organs. He screams in agony as the comp-ucube, adhering to its defensive protocol, destroys him from the inside out.

The comp-ucube lets out a deafening roar before flashing a white light that fills the entire room, blinding me and knocking me to the ground next to Shantelle's unconscious body. The shell of Khristoff's body falls to the floor in a loud clang along with the comp-ucube, which silences its growls into a lull of a purr.

Chapter 12

Tinkerverse

..

"But let each one test his own work, and then his
reason to boast will be in himself alone and not his
neighbor."

Galatians 6:4

..

The blinding light from the comp-ucube has the
same effect as the ricocheted lights of the East Sector
Club, magnified by a thousand percent. The sounds of
the comp-ucube's short-circuiting mechanical defense
are like the music scratched by a disc jockey who hides
in a dark and popular establishment. But the body odor
of the dancing teenagers who have spent the last
several hours gyrating in their own sweat cannot be
compared to the smell of Khristoff's charred remains.

In the corner of the East Sector Club, Thumbs sits
with Laci at his side. He stares out at the ever-moving
crowd, rubbing his throat from the stress of Uni's
deadly grip. Laci sits with a look of grave
disappointment, swiping through images on a portable
tablet of her sister when they both were at a healthy
weight.

"Let it go, Laci." Thumbs looks over his shoulder at
the tablet.

"It's easy for you." Laci lowers the device, raising
her voice over the music. "You don't have blood
family."

"Don't give me that!" He stares into her eyes with a

hint of evil. "Oscar shouldn't have interfered! If it wasn't for him, we'd have Uni's stash!"

"Do you even care that Anneli is dead?"

"You're missing the point!" He knocks the tablet from her hands and onto the table before them. "I did what was necessary. It was taking too long."

"Whatever." Laci turns in her seat, ignoring him.

"That's right, whatever." Thumbs looks out at the crowd with a growing smile. "If I oversaw SCS, I would have had Uni taken care of long ago. I would have removed his sales platform before he started that day. He would have shown up, and be like, where the hell did all my stuff go?" He throws his hands up, mocking Uni's confusion, and starts to chuckle.

"Grow up." Laci's attention returns to the tablet, keeping her eyes buried in her collection of memories.

"Like you care," he glances at her fingers as they navigate the system's file manager. "You wouldn't know what to do with complete power."

"Neither would you!" She looks up to prove a point.

"Yeah, I would! Who do you think taught me?" Thumbs keeps his glare solid.

"Well, it's not like he's sticking around to hold your hand."

"You're just jealous." He snaps.

"Shut up!"

The comp-uzync screen on his wrist flickers. Thumbs looks down with an annoyed reaction to the violent blinking, but his frown quickly curls into a smile.

"Speak of the devil. You said, 'Don't waste your time with After Dark.' Guess whose life insurance just paid off? I just inherited enough access codes to start a library."

From the other side of the East Sector Club, dancers in the middle of the room step across a dance floor of light and artificial smoke. Lasers of multicolored beams shoot out from the corners of the platform, flickering to the beat of the music. Shantelle appears near the front entrance, holding a small square object in one hand and clutching her stomach with the other. She stumbles through the crowd to the floating table where Thumbs and Laci are still arguing over who is right.

"Shantelle?" Laci looks her up and down. "Are you okay?"

"Yeah, babe. What happened to you?" Thumbs tries to act considerate, moving to the front side of the table to help Shantelle to the nearest seat.

"It was horrible!" Shantelle leans against a chair, balancing her weight while clutching the comp-ucube. "Sunder killed Khristoff."

"Are you serious?" Thumbs stands up straight, almost doubting the news. "What the hell happened?"

Shantelle adjusts her posture, holding the comp-ucube closer to her stomach. "Sunder did something to the cube."

"Are you okay?" Laci moves to Shantelle's side, rubbing the sides of her face.

"She's fine." Thumbs answers for her, following Shantelle's arm to the comp-ucube. "Did you bring it?"

"Damn it, Thumbs!" Laci snaps at him. "Can't you see that she's hurt?"

"Give it up," Thumbs orders.

"Why?" Shantelle coughs, clutching the comp-ucube closer.

"Because you don't know how to use it," he tries to sound sympathetic. "Let me show you."

Shantelle looks around the club and sees no reason to cause a scene by resisting him. She thinks over her weak condition in comparison to Thumbs who could most likely tear the comp-ucube from her clutches if he really wanted to.

She slowly offers the device which is quickly snatched up by the greedy young man. He spins it around in his hands, looking over the neuro-metal surface with enthusiasm. He smiles as he picks at the corner casing, discovering the transparent nanotube that extends like a retractable cord. He sticks out his tongue and is about to lick the end of the cable when Shantelle speaks up.

"Why should you get the cube?"

"Like you could do better." Thumbs looks Shantelle up and down, mocking her weak, semiconscious state.

"I bet you I could."

"Yeah, right, and I'm a gifted child with a registration form." He laughs to himself and continues to move the end of the tube toward his open mouth.

"She could." Laci steps up to Thumbs and pulls the tube from his hand.

"Are you serious?" He stares at Laci, gesturing to Shantelle as she awkwardly slumps down into the chair with both hands around her stomach. "She can't even sit up straight."

"She's better than you at everything."

"Oh, yeah?" He places the comp-cube on the table and the nanotube retracts with the sound of a winding zipper. "Prove it."

"She'll prove it." Laci looks at Shantelle with a sprouting smile. "Give her ten minutes. Then she'll show you what's up."

"Five," he holds up an open palm to haggle her terms. "I'll give her five minutes to prove me wrong."

"Deal!" Laci jumps from in front of Thumbs to Shantelle's chair. "Shantelle? What do you need? What can I get you?"

"I -- need -- my medicine." Shantelle speaks with a shortness in her breath.

"What kind of medicine? I can get you whatever you need." Laci tries to keep Shantelle's posture, wiping the sweat from her forehead.

"H -- D -- C -- V --" Shantelle's eyes slowly blink with each letter.

"What you need is a miracle." Thumbs overhears, mocking her with a smile.

"She needs a human diploid cell vaccine, genius." Laci glances back at Thumbs. "Get a degree."

"What is that supposed to mean?" He finds his seat on the other side of the table.

"It means, you have no ideas worth my time." Laci stretches her neck and looks out at the crowd, trying to spot the nearest waitress. "I need to flag her down."

"She's not going to help you." Thumbs crosses his arms, pessimistic about Laci asking for help from the blonde with blue eyeshadow.

"That's your problem." Laci stands from Shantelle's chair and rushes across the dance floor to the waitress carrying a tray of aqua-marbles.

Laci uses her expressive hands to illustrate the urgency of her request to the waitress, pointing back at the table where Shantelle slips in and out of awareness. The blonde waitress drops her jaw, nodding her head in an obvious reaction to a customer's medical need. She rushes away, almost dropping a half dozen marbles of water. Laci returns to Shantelle's side.

"What's going on?" Thumbs sounds interested in Laci's plight but does nothing to comfort Shantelle.

"I asked her for an Imovax."

"What? Im…O?"

"Seriously?" Laci sounds surprised, looking back at Thumbs. "It's a series of rabies vaccines created from samples of human cells."

"You better give her more than she needs. She'll need all the help she can get."

"It's amazing you can lead yourself to water," Laci mumbles as she helps Shantelle sit up in her seat. "Shantelle needs an injection every four days for two weeks in the affected area."

"You got all that from HDCV?"

"How did you ever get through school?"

"That's simple. I never went." Thumbs smiles to himself, thinking he is something special.

The blonde waitress returns on swift wheels, carrying a silver platter with one hand and balancing her weight with the other. She lowers the tray to Laci who reaches out and takes the syringe and bottle of HDCV. Laci fills the syringe and tosses the bottle across the table, shocking Thumbs out of his self-appreciating daydream.

"Hey -- careful!" Thumbs sits back, looking over the side of the table.

"Get a clue." Laci pulls out Shantelle's arm and violently stabs her in the shoulder, pushing the rabies vaccine into her bloodstream.

"Damn," Thumbs twitches in his seat as he watches. "Leave her an arm at least."

In a matter of minutes, the movement in Shantelle's eyes returns. As the disco lights revolve around the dance club, the strength in her legs brings her to an upright position. The dancers amid a hovering fog pay little attention to Shantelle as she slowly stands on her own. She pulls back her hair, looking around the club.

"I knew this was a bad idea," Shantelle secures her hair in a single bunch.

"Which part?" Thumbs crosses his arms. "Letting Sunny live, or letting Father die?"

"Coming here." Shantelle looks at Thumbs with a bit of resentment in her voice. "He's not the same guy you painted him to be."

"Sunny's a fool, and you're a fool for believing him." He slams his open hand on the table. "Whoever you are, Shantelle," he pauses, mocking her name. "He doesn't care about you." He slams his hand repeatedly, trying to illustrate his point. "He doesn't care about his daughter. He doesn't care about his wife, and he doesn't deserve this power!"

"Right. Like you do?"

"Hey!" Thumbs points at her. "I've seen enough to warrant this power. I've suffered enough to know what it feels like. You have no room to talk about loss. You're just a broken Willow."

"Don't call her that!" Laci speaks up. "She deserves respect! If it wasn't for her, that cube would still be outside."

"I don't have to take this from either of you." Thumbs reaches for the comp-ucube on the table. "I have the cube now, and it's all I need."

"That's what you always think about," Laci reaches out and grabs the comp-ucube before Thumbs has the chance. "Always yourself. Never anyone else."

"That cube belongs to me!" Thumbs holds out his open palm. "Give it to me!"

"You can't tell me what to do." Laci smirks, mocking Thumbs and his tantrum.

"I can." He presses a few buttons on his comp-uzync and a hologram display appears over the table between them. "You want to watch?"

"Whatever."

"Oh," Thumbs tilts his head upward to watch the hologram. "This is my favorite part."

Thumbs presses a button to tighten the viewing angle. The hologram shows Laci and Anneli talking to an older man in a quiet alleyway. His Silver Collar reflects the light from a nearby glass advertisement board. He smiles as Anneli hands him what only Laci and Thumbs would know is a transaction drive.

"I know what he's paying your sister for, but I'm sure it looks like just another backstage deal. I'll just add a juicy title."

"Why are you doing this?" Laci seems to be on the verge of breaking down in tears.

"I've suffered enough. Now, it's your turn." He refuses to look up from his rudimentary typing.

200

"It's not like I did this to you!" She shouts, unable to hold back her emotions.

"She's right!" Shantelle steps between Laci and Thumbs, taking the comp-ucube into her own hands. "I did this to you, and there's nothing you have against me."

"You got me there," Thumbs smiles, redirecting his stare to Shantelle. "I'll just tell SCS about your adventure inside the mainframe."

"Not to sound repetitive, but I don't have to give you anything." She tosses the comp-ucube in the air, catching it with the other hand. "Besides, you'd probably end up like your dad and smoke yourself to death."

"That won't happen."

"What makes you so sure about that?"

"Because" he crosses his arms. "The tale of the immortal man was never about Khristoff."

"What?" Laci interrupts.

Thumbs juggles his stares between Laci, Shantelle, and the comp-ucube. He licks his lips and scratches his chin, thinking of a way to get his hands involved. With a smile, he slaps his hands together.

"It's time to prove it," he points to Shantelle.

"Prove it?" Shantelle raises an eyebrow, looking back at Laci. "What's he talking about?"

"A challenge," Laci frowns, grabbing Shantelle's shoulder. "You can beat him."

"At what? Arm wrestling?" Shantelle suggests with a sarcastic tone. "It's not like I have an advantage."

"She's right. I don't play fair." Thumbs smiles at Laci. "But I'll let you choose the game."

"You're joking, right?" Laci lowers her head, keeping her gaze on Thumbs.

"Not at all." Thumbs crosses his arms. "You can set the rules, and I'll still win."

"What if we win?" Laci speaks up.

"If Shantelle wins? You can be in charge. You can tell everyone what to do. I'll never bother you again." He smiles, crossing his arms.

"And what happens if we lose?"

"I'll get the cube, and both of you have to do everything I say."

The music in the club continues through its playlist of popular songs, muffling out the conversation between the three absconders in the corner. Shantelle hands Laci the comp-ucube, which she tucks in the folds of her desert suit. Thumbs stands from his seat and makes his way onto the dance floor, waiting for Shantelle to join him. Shantelle takes her time, looking over the arcade games that line the perimeter of the East Sector Club.

She passes over several games that all seem too easy for Thumbs to win. She thinks about choosing a racing game but considers the lead Thumbs will have over her when the starting light turns green. She wonders if Thumbs will turn out to have better aim as she muses over a first-person shooter. Could she beat him at dancing with two left feet and fighting to keep her own neck from breaking? Then Laci points to a recipe game on the opposite side of the club.

"There's your game!" Laci shouts over the music, nudging Shantelle in the same direction.

"Tinkerverse?" Thumbs throws his head back in a chuckle. "Yeah, sure. I'll take you on. It's all skill that you don't have."

Shantelle thinks back to the absconder camp where trinkets and mechanics riddled the ground like incomplete robotic projects. She remembers the floor of the Suite Oasis and the tools she used to fix the compression engine. She looks at the arcade game and studies the decals of gears and wires that cover the outside of the large machine, smiling at her odds of winning.

Thumbs enters his name into the Tinkerverse system log and Shantelle does the same. A splash message appears on the tiny screen, offering two versions of the same game. Rather than play a local two-dimensional simulation, Thumbs insists he and Shantelle take a step back. As the game's internal music starts, a group of nearby dancers adjust their routine by distancing themselves from the two young absconders who just locked their names into a serious battle. The music of the club slowly fades out and the hidden disc jockey makes an announcement.

"Listen up, now," he starts with a quick, loud tone. "We got ourselves a face-off!" He drops the beat, and his charismatic message continues over the dampening music. "Let's clear the dance floor -- clear the dance floor! That means you too, sexy. And let's bring up the sub-ar-eee-na! You're in for a special treat. Let's turn up the fog!"

A fog-encrusted beam of light is projected onto

Shantelle's head, encasing her cranium in a weightless electronic blanket. The shape of a helmet materializes over her tousled orange hair, creating a series of sensors that are able to pinpoint her thoughts. Teenagers cheer, taking their places surrounding the perimeter of the sub-floor arena where Shantelle and Thumbs stand amid a holographic projection of a mechanical workshop. Designed within the floor to use holographic cameras and projection lenses, Tinkerverse allows its players to create a fully manipulative universe.

The disc jockey continues.

"Let's go over the rules. For each round, players are given the same ingredients, the same materials, and the same components. The player who configures the better device wins the point."

The crowd erupts in hoots and hollers. Men and women alike throw up their hands, stomping their bare feet on the illuminated dance floor. The word TINKERVERSE appears in the fog that spills from a machine above them, and then disappears. The words ROUND 1 appear, followed by the words MOBILE SURVEILLANCE. As the fog continues to pour over the arena, a plethora of digitally rendered components appears around the players.

Shantelle recognizes several items that are displayed around her. She holds out a hand and selects an antenna, dragging the image across the fog to a connection block. She adds a motion sensor and a power cell from another group of components. While she selects a sound transmitter, a visual scanner, and a circuit board for the data relay, Thumbs is doing the same on his own assembly line.

A buzzer chimes over the cheering crowd, and the time has come for the players to reveal their devices. Shantelle finishes the last connection on her surveillance unit and displays to the crowd a versatile, multi-legged creature that can travel over rough terrain to monitor any subject. The crowd around her erupts in a heckle and a cheer. Thumbs displays his device as a maneuverable winged creature in the shape of a bat that can cover large distances with a broader viewing spectrum. The crowd shouts in mixed reviews. The disc jockey returns to the microphone.

"Both players look confident in their devices but from the sound of the crowd," he pauses. "Looks like the point goes to the bat!"

Dancers stomp their feet and clap their hands, patting Thumbs on the back for a well-earned point. With a smile, he waves his hand across the holographic display, erasing the round and adding his point to the scoreboard. The words ROUND 2 appear in the fog, which to Shantelle is a depressing sight. She looks up with heavy shoulders, remembering the Hyltots outside the Oasis, believing she should have won. The fog fills with the words, SURVIVAL GEAR, the theme of the second challenge.

The assembly line around Shantelle disappears and quickly reappears with a new arrangement of digitally rendered components. She reaches for an air compressing chamber and exhale valve, thinking with a smile on how she will win the next point. She adds a heating and cooling unit to her connection block, configuring the circuit board with a filter coil and control switch. While Thumbs configures the schematics for a hydro-generator, Shantelle finishes with the detailed plans of her gas mask. The disc jockey calls out as the buzzer chimes.

"Alright! Let's see what's going on!"

Thumbs powers the hydro-generator that produces an impressive amount of water for its size. The crowd around him screams for his winning design. Shantelle funnels her gas mask with a huge cloud of smoke, and it releases copious amounts of fresh oxygen. The crowd around her screams louder than those who want Thumbs to win.

"Whoa!" The disc jockey cries out through the speakers. "We've got a tied game! Point goes to the gas mask! I guess I'm not the only one who likes breathing."

The crowd erupts in laughter, clapping for Shantelle's winning point. With a look of betrayal across his face, Thumbs violently waves both hands through the fog, erasing the assembly line display and adding Shantelle's point to the scoreboard.

"Let's keep things going!" The disc jockey starts his music that overpowers the roaring voice of the crowd. "We've got the third round coming up! Don't go away!"

Thumbs approaches Shantelle and Laci from across the dance floor, glaring at them through the fog that keeps them hidden from those outside the illuminated sub-floor arena. He ignores the people around them who smile and share handshakes over the game that has taken the entire club by popular force.

"It's just a point." Thumbs takes a step closer to Laci. "But the game's not over."

"Then why the fear?" Laci smiles, seeing through his trials to cover his shame.

"What fear?" He holds up his hands and looks around. "I run all this!"

"Not anymore." Shantelle speaks with a stern look.

The strobe lights flicker to the music and the rotating beams of color that dance against the mirrored surface of the walls bleed faster. The music slowly fades out and the disc jockey's voice returns over the crowd of mixed reviews.

"Contestants ready!"

"I'm ready to kick you out of Thicket!" Thumbs addresses Shantelle from across the dance floor, letting his voice carry through the illuminated fog.

Shantelle refuses to show any emotion to Thumbs or the crowd. She simply nods her head at the disc jockey who proceeds to continue their game. The fog thickens around the players and the words ROUND 3 appear and quickly fade out, followed by the word NAVIGATION. An assembly line appears around Shantelle and Thumbs, showcasing dozens of digitally rendered compass parts.

Shantelle looks around her assembly table, thinking back to what her mother taught her. As she connects the pieces of the compass to the connection block, she recalls a lesson on the planet's magnetic field. She adds the needle to point its navigator to magnetic north but then remembers the heavy ice storm that covered most of the planet, reversing its polarity. Because Thumbs never went to school, he would never know such a minor detail in the planet's history.

"Well, it looks like they're starting to think alike." The disc jockey continues over the suspenseful music. He highlights both players and their compass designs. "But let's see which one works better!"

The crowd erupts in a tempo of clapping.

"On the count of three, players, turn on your instruments! Uno! Zwei! Threeeee!"

At the sound of the number three, both Shantelle and Thumbs flip a holographic switch on their navigation devices. Their needles spin in circles several times, wiggling until they stop moving, pointing in opposite directions.

"See!" Thumbs smiles, pointing at Shantelle's compass. "You can't even make a basic compass work! What good are you?"

Shantelle keeps her answer hidden behind a subtle frown.

The disc jockey shines a spotlight on the needle of both devices.

"It looks like one of these devices is not up-to-date." He addresses the crowd, pointing out that only one compass can be correct. "Do you all want a boring history lesson?"

"No!" The crowd shouts back.

"Fair enough." He quickly changes the tone in his voice. "Round 3 goes to the girl!"

"What?" Thumbs shouts over the cheering crowd. "Impossible!"

"That's what a lack of education will do to you," Laci speaks up.

The crowd cheers for Shantelle from all sides of the club. Numerous waitresses circle the dance floor taking drink orders as Shantelle takes the lead. Thumbs watches a waitress roll toward him to an encouraging table on the other side of the club. He purposely trips her, letting her service tray skip across the illuminated dance floor, spilling aqua-marbles of various colors.

"Double or nothing!" Thumbs shouts over the profane taunts of the nearby club goers who disagree with his behavior.

"No way," Shantelle points. "You can lose fair and square like a normal person."

"Double or nothing, or I destroy her forever." Thumbs presses a button on his comp-uzync, illustrating the air above his implant with a three-dimensional memory of Shantelle and her mother.

"You wouldn't." She stares at Thumbs through the likeness of her mother in the electronic haze of evaporated water.

"I would," he corrects her. "And if I were you, I'd give up."

"You're never going to win." She clenches a fist and waves her other hand over the fog, resetting the assembly line and adding her second point to the scoreboard.

The words ROUND 4 appear in the holographic fog and quickly fade out, followed by the word JIP. The disc jockey lowers the volume of the music, speaking out over the crowd.

"Round four, people! Tiny Tim homeless is still in the game." He pushes a button and the strobe lights and rotating colors freeze. "Let's see if he can regain control of the scoreboard." In the sudden rush of moving lights, the teenagers around the dance floor begin moving hysterically in one big circle around the contestants. Thumbs smiles over the category of the round, having recently learned to manipulate his own Jip mask. Shantelle smiles, but feels nervous, having never used a face shield in her life.

Thumbs starts to assemble an interface, threading the component for a fiber optic cable through a sheet of polarized glass. Taking the time to draw a tiny heart in the pane of electronic glass, he smiles at Shantelle who is still deciding on the first component to add to her connecting block.

Thumbs throws up his hands. The crowd cheers,

clapping for a countdown to his victory. He gestures to the disc jockey to start the music.

Shantelle tries her best by using the components that look convincing for a pair of visors. Without the necessary electrical current, powered by the fiber optic cable, her Jip mask will simply be a pair of reading frames. As beads of sweat begin to form on her forehead, the music in the club intensifies, coinciding with the countdown from the crowd around her.

"Time's up, babe!" Thumbs shouts over the music as he announces his win to the crowd. "These are all my points. I'm only lending you the ones I don't need now."

"Players!" The disc jockey speaks. "Let's see who will be on top!"

As part of the game, the final components for the round float in the holographic display above each player. The face shield above Thumbs illuminates in a bright orange cloud of static, showcasing a recorded video of Thumbs in the East Sector Club. The visors above Shantelle, illuminated in a bright pink cloud of static, does not display anything.

"Yes!" Thumbs throws his arms outward and his head back in laughter. "Yes, yes, yes."

"We have a winner!" The jockey announces.

"That's not fair!" Laci points to Thumbs. "He's connected to it! He's feeding it footage!"

"Thanks for playing!" The jokey lowers the volume to Tinkerverse's musical scoreboard and returns to his normal sequence of popular music.

"Don't be ridiculous." Thumbs moves close to Laci. "Just admit you lost. You're jealous of my skills. I can construct more with my eyes closed than you'll ever understand."

Thumbs gestures to the shield above him, lowering them to Laci's eye level. He pushes them toward her. "Take a look."

"No!" Laci waves her hand, launching them on Shantelle's face, covering her eyes.

Shantelle's face becomes digitally rendered for a few moments, illuminating the dance floor with a flash of bright orange. In a moment of panic, she pushes the mask off, which disappears with the rest of the game's fog-light components. Her legs buckle and she falls to the floor, holding her head with both hands and crying out in pain.

"See what I mean!" Thumbs hears the energetic crowd shouting his name. "You can never beat me," holding up his hands. "All drinks on me!"

Laci tries to hold back her anger. She approaches Thumbs, swinging her fist into his shoulder, as if struggling to accept his immature behavior.

"You're a monster."

Thumbs turns around, catching Laci's fist, and backhands her to the floor. He reaches down and takes the comp-ucube from the folds of her desert suit, leaving her curled in the fetal position.

An older boy from the crowd rushes to Shantelle's

side, helping her to stand. He supports her weight as she slowly walks to a nearby seat. Tucking the strands of hair covering her face behind her ears, he asks if there is anything he can do to ease the pain.

"What happened?" She keeps her eyes lowered.
"His Jip mask blinded you. Are you okay?" He tries his best to make her comfortable.
"I don't know." Shantelle looks around, unable to recall any flash of light.

The scoreboard above the crowd lingers in the fog with the tally of points. Shantelle looks up at her name appearing in a smaller font, resonating as one of the players.

"Tinkerverse? I want to watch."

The older boy's eyes widen.

Thumbs moves to the floating table in the corner with the comp-ucube in his hands. He holds up the device to the crowd that continues to shout his name. With a boastful smile he extends the transparent nanotube from the corner of the comp-ucube and quickly coats the end with a mouthful of saliva. He glances back at Shantelle before he inserts the tube into the side of his implant.

Within seconds, the transparent nanotube turns into a kaleidoscope of colors, floating upward, while the air surrounding Thumbs and the comp-ucube thickens with the smell of heated metal. The casing of the comp-ucube begins to glow red and resonate with a loud purr. Thumbs closes his eyes and smiles, relaxing his shoulders with the energy that flows out from the tiny device.

"What's he doing?" Shantelle asks the older boy, staring intently across the dance floor at Thumbs with sincere confusion.

"I don't know," he stands from her side. "But he's not going to get away with it."

The older boy rushes in, raising his clenched fists, pulling back his weight. He lunges forward to tackle Thumbs, hoping to knock the comp-ucube from his grip. He tries to catch Thumbs in the booth of the suspended table and beat him with the vindication Shantelle deserves. He swings with his left fist. Thumbs opens his eyes which appear electrically bright, and with a solid shift in weight, he avoids the punch. His shoulders flex, and he punches the older boy in the face, breaking his nose.

"Who the hell do you think you are?" The older boy holds his nose, hoping to contain the blood that is dripping onto the dance floor.

"I'm the Father now." His voice is galvanizing and deep, echoing like thunder in a metallic drum.

Chapter 13

Heal with Time

..

"The iniquities of the wicked ensnare him, and he is held fast in the cords of his sin. He dies for lack of discipline, and because of his great folly he is led astray."

Proverbs 5:22-23

..

The Suite Oasis is more than a hydro-filtration plant. It also stands as a rudimentary link to the city of Thicket. The room that houses the vital machinery for the city's water supply is now the same room that contains the burnt remains of Khristoff Dakya.

I wake in a daze to the pungent smell of Khristoff's carcass. A thin layer of smoke still lingers in the air, invading my nasal cavity more as I stand. I look around the room, collecting my scattered memories of the monster's demise. The first thing I can recall is the impression of Jessica's face, masked in the compulsive persona of Shantelle's alter ego. She gambled with my own freedom for a chance to help manipulate the people of Thicket.

I do not want to believe that my daughter could be a habitual liar, but then I suddenly start to follow the symptoms of Willow Amnesia and what Laci was trying to tell me. Willow Amnesia is an irreversible disease that Shantelle will never escape. She wakes up every morning living the memories of other people. Some people call this hereditary disease by the ghost that resides within the machine. Other people call it karma for having a natural birth while tampering with the subconscious on a technological high.

I am unable to accept that Shantelle is just a junkie, runaway version of my daughter. It is an unbearable realization that my daughter exists solely as a random surprise to a girl who is not in the slightest bit interested in her family's existence.

In my tortured imagination, I create a slew of caricatures. Envisioning a crazy day for each decade; I see an abnormal tempest, a woman in transparent attire, and an irrational teenager, harnessed like a farmer's pet. The farmer's hair rotates in color, as well as her eyes. For a moment I think I see Jessica and I call out her name. Am I merely looking for Shantelle?

I search behind each working machine, calling out her name, but find no trace of Shantelle or Jessica, or the comp-ucube. The entry-port to the link-rail pod is open and the transport is missing from its cradle. Still trying to adjust to the smell, I realize that Shantelle has fled to the city on the link-rail with the comp-ucube in her possession.

Among the tools and mechanics of Khristoff's workshop, the remains of a desert suit wardrobe litter the floor. To my benefit, a pair of sturdy goggles have been left near some neuro-metal boots and synthetic skin gloves. In addition to the portable hydro-generator we found at the absconder camp, I will need these accessories if I am to get back to the city alive.

My thoughts parade in my head as I change my boots and slip on the pair of gloves. I think about Sherianne and the day we discovered we were going to be parents as I stretch the goggles over my forehead. When I approach the entry-port to the wasteland, I think about my daughter and the creature she turned out to be.

There is more to Shantelle's personality than I may want to understand. She traded in her own life, changed her hair color, and buried the past that eventually led her back to her family. The entry-port opens with the pull of a lever and the hot desert winds of the midday sun enter the suite, nudging me into taking a step back.

The essence of the wasteland is not as strong as the smell emitting from Khristoff's body. With my desert suit hood wrapped tightly around my head and my goggles secured in place, I take a step toward the western horizon.

For more than 10 hours I hike in a single direction, hoping to reuse the path I previously forged. The storms of the wasteland have covered the footprints that Shantelle and I carved along the way, but I am able to recognize a mountain of rubble that looks to contain the pieces of an entire neighborhood. I think I am going the right way.

I venture through an asphalt sea of mangled shopping carts and a graveyard of toppled automobiles. Staring at the potential of transportation laying in ruin, I consider the chances of fixing a piece of outdated technology, shaking my head at the reality that I know nothing about it.

From opposite angles, I observe the hills and mountain peaks that could have surrounded the absconder camp. I then notice the structures that have been worn down by lightning strikes and acidic rain.

The absconder camp on Paiute Mountain is empty, and the last of the refugee's equipment was either dismantled or confiscated by SCS, leaving nothing behind that could benefit a survivor. Hoping to quench my thirst, I operate the hydro-generator, but find it malfunctioning. I now feel like I am running low on luck. There are no transports in the area, nor are there any modes of communication with the city. I sense that I am walking abandoned.

I feel the need to rest, but with clear skies on the horizon, I search the structures for any piece of useful equipment. In several make-shift homes, I find the family portraits of those who fled the area. Painted in oil and clay, the portraits render each facial expression in murky colors of the barren earth.

Standing in the middle of Crowchest, I feel the same pain I did all those years ago. This is where Sherianne lived. Shantelle was trying to tell me something and now I feel as though I am deserting them once again.

As the sun starts to crest the top of the horizon, I feel I can no longer waste my time in this forsaken wasteland if I am to find out what happened to

Shantelle and the comp-ucube. I must take the direct trail to the city without stopping for sleep.

After several hours of walking through hills of cracked desert and sun-dried debris in the twilight, I can feel the effects of hunger and malnutrition. As I reach into my desert suit to retrieve the cylindrical container, I trip over the chrome bumper of a buried automobile and launch my Cau-li supply into the air. The container crashes into the side of a sunken boulder and my presses spill through the cracks in the ground. The rattle of my Cau-li presses echo on their way to the bottom of the buried pickup truck.

My heart falls to the dry earth. The last of my food supply drops like marbles on a tall staircase. I feel the last of my strength escaping my grip as I claw at the cold sand below me.

As the sun sinks below the horizon, painting the desert around me in darkness, my heart prays for the silhouette of the city's perimeter. Like a mirage on the desert's skyline, I want to be convinced by such an illusion. All hope cannot be lost, but I struggle to give into the setting of betrayal. I need to march on. With each step, the pain in my leg worsens and the weight of my body tumbles forward.

I tell myself I must keep going. I cannot give up all that I have accomplished. Having a hard time accepting my fate, I feel as though I cannot let Shantelle go without releasing my daughter, her hostage, nor can I let the comp-ucube fall into the hands of SCS. If I can just make it back to the city, the pain in my leg and burning in my throat will pass. I tell myself, it will all be over soon.

I hear from my comp-uzync an ever-increasing warning bell, alerting me to the fact that my vitals are starting to fail. The end is coming early.

The horizon pulls away from me in sparkles of a dark hue. Before my entire view is swallowed up by fatigue and pain, I make out the face of my wife. Standing in front of me as beautiful as the day I met her, I watch as Sherianne takes me by the hand.

My consciousness falls deeper than sleep. I feel lost in a maze of uncertain results, constantly correcting my actions with assumptions of guilt and disease. In the distance I see my daughter, running away from her past. I recognize the mirage for what the desert wants to show me, a glimpse into my own reality. The girl that looks to be Shantelle is holding onto the hand of a boy near her age. I can only presume they have fallen in love.

The love that I feel for Jessica quickly dissolves. She is no longer the little girl I considered as family. I can only see her now as a wanderer, an absconder, a shell of a memory that was designed to remain. In my distortion, I watch as she runs in my direction, but further and further away, always out of my reach. Headed into the sunrise of another day, the vision of Shantelle blinds me in my fatigue. Hoping for my vision to return, I no longer see Shantelle, but rather the face of a young man with a bloody nose, holding onto my feet as he drags me over rocks and sand.

Suddenly, the decay of the wasteland is no longer a concern. I wake to the sight of someone hovering over me. Cradled on the neuro-metal pavement where a crowd whispers and gawks, a dreamlike face meets my own to help me sit up.

From behind me, a hand holds the back of my head. I feel a cold metal injection in the side of my neck and my eyes flicker open. Another hand feeds a cauliflower press to my open mouth.

"What do you think you're doing?" Someone squeezes my shoulder to get a reflex. "How long have you been out there?"

I swallow the press that I so desperately need and cough, looking around at the people who stand in groups of murmuring conversations.

"I thought I still was --" I look around, squinting.
"Are you delirious? Where have you been?"

I blink a few more times, trying to get my focus to return. I rub my forehead and look again, contempt with seeing Arlita at my aid.

"Khristoff's dead." I roll onto my side. "Jessica has the cube and she's somewhere in the city." I try to stand. "I have to get it back."
"Jessica?" She tries to help but just watches me get up slowly. "She's alive?"
"You tell me, Lita." I respond sarcastically, walking away from her. "You saw her and didn't tell me."

"I told you what you needed to hear. I saw an aura around a young girl, and I assumed that she was someone you forgot." Arlita walks after me in her argument. "It was up to you to decide how important she was. You found your daughter on your own. Where are you going?"

"I don't know," I huff as I turn around. "Something's not right. I just -- I need to go." I start to leave.

"To see the priest?"

"How did you --" I do not sound assured.

"There was an emergency. He's been taken to Medic Tower. Someone found him asleep on the altar with his comp-uzync cracked."

"Cracked?" My words sound stunned. "Sleeping?"

At the northern edge of the marketplace, the Medical Sector is where the people of Thicket come to repair their physical demands. Whether someone is injured by blunt trauma, mistreated by malnutrition, or appears ugly on the outside and prefers the look of plastic surgery, the Medic Tower is here in the form of government aid.

The curved buildings to either side of the Tower are the Alpha and Beta Medical Wings, designated for outpatient housing and extensive private research. The Silver Collar Society takes care of its citizens, treating every registered body the same. They can also accommodate the highest bidder and monopolize research funding. I hold my breath when we walk in.

The entry-port to the Tower is inviting, but the lack of a human presence does not seem right to me. I feel

222

as though the first step in helping a person through a painful ordeal should be another human to empathize the experience. Instead, a large digital directory board is displayed to direct us to the appropriate floor.

Treatments for malnutrition are assigned to the first five floors. Appointments for various types of cosmetic surgery are assigned to the next ten floors. As we walk toward the elevators, I can feel the pain in my leg returning. I try to regain my composure. Breathing in and out, I hope the day will not continue in a downward pattern.

I look at the reflected mirror's edge and see the aging face of regret. I see a painfully notable receding hairline and the large earlobes that match my square chin. I feel as if my age is catching up to me, wanting to find a bed to lay in and sleep for the next few hundred years.

Arlita presses a button on the elevator, turning to me as if I deserve an explanation.

"I'm sorry."
"For what?" I glance at her as I watch the elevator's numbers go up.
"I should have told you about Jessica."

The elevator door opens, and I notice a couple of Collars standing outside one of the medical rooms. I place a hand on Arlita's shoulder, walking past her.

They cross their arms when I approach.

223

"Excuse me --" I clear my throat. "Is this Miko's room?"

"No authorization." One Collar speaks in a German accent.

"No visitors." The other Collar translates in Russian.

My confused gaze bounces between the two of them.

"Well," I move for Arlita, positioning her between me and the two men. "I brought his mother. They haven't seen each other in quite a while."

"Yes," Arlita adds, deciding to play along. "You'll make an exception for his mother, won't you? I would like to know what happened to my son."

"I'm sorry, ma'am, but we've been given direct orders."

"I beg your pardon." Arlita blinks her eyes with a deep, raspy tone in her voice.

"Nothing personal, ma'am," the other tries to sympathize with her. "We can't let anyone in. Authorized personnel only."

"Can I speak to you for a second?" I gesture for him to step to the side. "Do you know what'll happen to Miko if he dies without his mother at his side?"

"Not my concern." He pulls his shoulders back, widening his chest.

"Well, it should be." I steal a glance at Arlita and the other Collar still standing in front of the room. "He's the only one who knows what happened and the person responsible for this is still out there. It'll look bad on your part if this happens again, and they order you with the same detail. This isn't the best

224

assignment, now is it?"

"Is that right? Civilian?"

I look down, feeling as if I must confront this misunderstanding with my own intelligence and wit.

"I'm saying, before I take my own final vows for the church," I thoughtfully invent. "I need to exorcise true grit." I calmly hold up my pressed palms.

His arms seem to shake loose as I start to gain his interest.

"You know how much pent-up anger is left between these two?" I approach Arlita and hold her next to me, gesturing for her to sell my story with the innocent smile of a victim. "She's got so much lecturing left to do."

The German Collar agrees with a humble chuckle. I guess he finds the thought of a priest being scolded by his mother the same as the magic word. He turns and signals the other Collar to step aside and let us enter the post-operation room.

The small metallic door opens into a high-tech medical room, where Miko rests in a bed with several active machines around him. One machine monitors his heart rate while another administers an intravenous dosage of pain relief.

The Silver Collar priest's bed is raised off the floor, extending from the wall like a medical tongue. Miko rests under a plastic blanket that regulates his body

225

temperature. His face is bruised and wrapped in white cloth. Only his eyes and mouth are visible, with a tube inserted in his nose.

"Priest," the German Collar speaks into the room. "You have a visitor."

"Thank you." I walk back to follow him out. "We won't be long."

He nods and closes the door behind him.

I approach Miko's bed, rustling the plastic blanket. Arlita moves to the foot of the bed, refusing to touch the structure as if her touch would be too much for the bed's weight capacity.

"Alright, Miko --" I touch the priest's shoulders. "Miko, wake up."

Slowly, the priest opens his eyes and blinks as if he is afraid.

"What happened? Who did this to you?" I pull the blanket off and see that most of his body is covered in bandages.
"People -- danger --" With a machine to regulate his breathing between each other word, Miko is barely able to speak above a whisper.
"You knew what Khristoff wanted all along, didn't you?"

Miko's eyes freeze at the sound of the question. His hands, which are also bandaged, slowly come up to shield his Collar. His comp-uzync is heavily destroyed, showcasing a crack in the screen that reminds me of the stalagmites of Paiute Mountain.

"Khristoff --" He takes a long, deep breath. "-- wants -- cube --"

"Shantelle took the cube." I look to Arlita for help but find nothing of value in her blank stare. "Where did Shantelle take the cube?"

"Children -- save --" He points to his heart.

"Save who? My daughter?" My eyes trace the white bandages around his face as my questions go unanswered.

"Tried --" he shakes his head. "-- choice --"

"What choice? She came to you for help." I lean closer, almost able to smell the blood and infection through the soaked bandages. "What did you do to her?"

The priest shakes his head in tears, mumbling into his bandaged hands. The words he speaks are inaudible to Arlita, but as a father figure, I am able to understand the violent betrayal in Miko's voice. I hear the words INJECT and WILLOW and I picture Shantelle wandering back to the cathedral where she thought she would be safe. She would never have known the bargain placed against her return. She would never have anticipated the priest's intentions.

"What were you thinking, old man?" I grind my teeth together as I speak. "How could you do that to my daughter? I trusted you. What were you expecting to get from her?

"A heart --" Arlita adds, no longer keeping silent at

the foot of Miko's bed.

"Khristoff should have killed you when he had the chance. I should have."

"Sunder!" Arlita calls. "He needs a heart transplant."

"What?" I take a breath, slowly my thoughts as if altering my judgment. "A transplant?" My focus moves to the bandaged hand covering Miko's heart.

I slowly step away from the medical bed, joining the view of the window while remembering the way Miko clutched his chest as we spoke in the cathedral. I hold my silence with my arms crossed and an intent of dislike gleaming behind my eyes. I try hard to understand the need of a young heart, and the benefits weighed between saving the old versus the young.

"Sunder, listen to me." Arlita tries with reason, joining me at the window. "You can't get your daughter back. She's not the same person you left in that camp. Whatever you do can't bring back the past. All we can do is accept our fate and move along for the sake of others. Besides," she looks back at Miko who is crying behind his bandages. "What ever happened to Khristoff is probably what he deserved."

"As a child, he didn't deserve to be sacrificed." I stare at Miko.

"As your child?" Arlita adds. "How much would you allow? Does a parent sympathize for their child who doesn't want to remember home?"

I take in a deep breath, first looking at the neuro-metal boots that support my weight and then up to Arlita who tries to break my concentration with a friendly smile.

Arlita moves to Miko's bed, kneels, and takes his closest hand into her own. She pulls his bandaged wrist to her lips and kisses the white cloth, whispering into the fabric.

"My dearest Lord. Please watch over your lost sheep. Protect your flock from the temptations of evil. Look after your followers with the same love you deserve. Although a lost soul may not be worthy of your grace, I pray for this beaten man. Let his soul be welcome into your house of love. May his sins be forgiven and his conscious be cleansed. I ask this through our Lord, and Savior."

Arlita stands from Miko's bed and returns to me. With a smile, she walks past and opens the door to find the two Collars still at their post. I take one last look at Miko before departing his room and leaving the priest to his own conscious understanding. I think about his heart surgery and the donor needed to have a successful operation.

Miko's condition seems like a devious scheme that will forever plague his face, if only visible in his watering eyes and quivering lips. I want to know more about whatever happened in the cathedral, but I figure that something this traumatic has no room for descriptive words. I close the door behind me, letting the old man whimper alone.

"He should be fine." Arlita addresses the Collars with a gentle wave as she walks me to the elevator.

"He'll heal with time."

They nod in agreement, crossing their arms as they listen in on the tail-end mummer of Miko's whimpering.

As Arlita and I ride the elevator to the bottom floor, I wonder about the brief dialogue that Miko was not able to finish. I wonder about the words Arlita whispered over the priest's bed, and I wonder about the revenge that sent such violence to the city cathedral.

"Who do you think he was talking about?" I turn to face Arlita in the elevator.

"The donor? Or the children?" Arlita shrugs her shoulders. "Could have been any number or them. I see signs everywhere."

"Signs," I look away in thought. "But who would seek revenge like that?"

"Don't worry about it." She reaches out to touch my shoulder as the elevator door opens to the bottom floor. "What else can you do? Slap their wrist for protecting their friend?"

I agree with a look of sympathy and walk away from the Medic Tower with Arlita at my side. The crowded streets are not as packed now that the sun is going down. The night brings out a different set of pedestrians who stay in the shadows and alleyways, giving us more room to walk freely down the street.

The air at night smells cleaner and the lights from nearby billboards look brighter. It seems that the city of Thicket is more perfect without its people plaguing the streets. The walk back to Arlita's apartment is quick and comforting. Neither one of us must push or shove our way through or tell a single vendor that we are not interested in their merchandise. When Arlita approaches the entry-port to her apartment, I stop short.

"There's one thing that still bothers me." I look at the control panel on the entry-port. "If Khristoff's dead, who'd want the cube?"

"Sunder --" Arlita speaks with a sigh. "Do you remember the dedication ceremony?"

"Yeah, what about it?"

"The prophecy was never about Loy. The signs are happening again, and I've seen them in the streets," she strolls her stoop.

"What do you mean? Another uprising?"

"Haven't you seen the abundance of children these days? They all seem to be running in the same mindset. They're stealing and dealing, occupying and ordering. I think they're preparing for another shift in power."

"Well, like you said." I tilt my head while rubbing my hairline. "We shouldn't worry about it unless there's something we can do about it." I back away as if I am requesting my leave. "I just need a good night's sleep."

Arlita smiles and waves me on my way. She opens the entry-port to her apartment and lets it close behind her. I zip up the folds of my desert suit out of habit, looking around for anyone else still awake. Wondering where all the children sleep as I walk around dimly lit corners, I pass exhaust vents and think about the families torn apart from the raid on the wasteland camps. Can the city really be the only logical hope for

231

the survival of their children?

The neon green light from the link-rails above is bright enough to illuminate my path. Accustomed to the same footsteps from previously visiting Arlita's apartment for guidance and walking home, I feel reacquainted with the assurance in what she had to say. The link-rails in the Triennial Division travel in two directions, transporting dozens of insomniacs and those who function better at night, and rather than return to the privileged apartments of the West Sector, I decide to expand my curiosity and venture further into the night.

I walk to the nearest link-rail station and board the next available pod, taking an empty seat next to a young blonde girl with streaks of pale green in her hair. The transport is crowded with several children in the company of one, barely-made adult. The sight of their youth brings a smile to my heart but sparks my intuition of concern. These children are most likely involved in this new revolution that Arlita mentioned, and any one of them could be responsible for Miko's broken form.

I see the tallest one of the group as their leader, wearing the bloody bandage of a broken nose. I watch a tiny child curl up as if either cold or afraid of the calm in the air. Assuming the worst of their situation, I check in.

"You all sleep here?" I look around the transport in acknowledgment of the limited room to lay flat.
"We stay with our Father." The young girl flips her

blonde hair, revealing a set of pink lips tattooed on the side of her neck.

The sight of the same tattoo changes nothing in my mood. The other children on the transport glare at me in my attempt at talking to someone who is trying to sleep.

I stand and move to another seat as the transport speeds on its way across the city. The other children who sit around me know nothing of my endeavor or the circumstances of the immortal man in the Suite Oasis. They whisper to each other while exchanging glances of an applied rumor. One of the children in the corner of the transport smiles and I can read his lips.

He calls me a loser.

Chapter 14

Main Investment

..

"Because you did not serve the Lord your God with joyfulness and gladness of heart, because of the abundance of all things, therefore you shall serve your enemies whom the Lord will send against you, in hunger and thirst, in nakedness, and lacking everything. And he will put a yoke of iron on your neck until he has destroyed you."

Deuteronomy 28:47-48

..

The transport travels through miles of link-rail tubes, commuting me and a group of homeless children across the city. To anyone walking on the streets below, the pod seems to be working properly, but to myself who sits in silence, surrounded by the newest generation of absconder youth, the pod is not going fast enough.

The older boy stands up, easing his resting friend into the shoulder of another sleeping body. His face seems familiar, like a vision from a dream, but his stride shows attitude that makes him older than the severity of his broken nose. He sits next to the sleeping girl, introducing himself as her protection.

"Should I?" He squints his eyes.
"You don't have to tell me anything." I keep my voice and movements to a hush, directing my gaze elsewhere. "And I don't have to drag you outside."

Channeling the memory of my encounter with the bouncer, I try my best remain calm. Remembering the sleight of hand from the blonde waitress, I stand from my seat and move toward the windowpane.

"Just remember. It'll come back," I mumble.

I tuck my fists into the front pockets of my suit and find the lining filled. As I pull out and unfold the portrait of Sherianne, an object tumbles onto the floor of the transport. Pondering the luck that no longer exists over the risk of getting caught with the damning evidence, I reach for what I recognize as my missing Imprint Drive.

The young man with the broken nose jumps to his feet and quickly snatches what he will now defend as trash.

"Uh oh," he smirks.
"Not going to happen," I extend my open palm, demanding he return the drive.
"What was that word?" He turns the ID over. "Losers, weepers."
"If I were you --"
"I'm pretty adamant about who I am," he casually takes the folded parchment from my hands and unfolds it. "But she could be."

Understanding biological urges, I can never find fault in a teenager's mindset. Knowing that he recognizes Sherianne is simply another mirror in my attempt at discovering the truth. I think about the value I placed on something that has done nothing for me.

With a clear desire in my life, I release my fixation on control and lower my hand.

"You know what," I smile. "Keep it."
"Did I make a request?"
"Do yourself a favor," I gesture to the blood from his broken nose. "Set an example."

I start to think that he will refuse to take me seriously by the way he chuckles through his smile. With an accepted nod in agreement on my part and an informal acceptance of sarcasm on his, I step onto the rotating platform of a passing link-rail station and let the transport continue its path through the city.

The streets between the North Alpha and North Beta Sectors are quiet and the marketplace is empty. Anyone awake at this hour is either hiding in the shadows, dealing in dark market sales, or assisting with unauthorized surgeries. The oxygen vents that bellow steam from its grates and gutters are the only mechanical sounds I hear as I follow my memory through the alleyways of Thicket. I expect to find a Collar patrolling the streets but feel alone in my travels.

I turn one corner and follow another alleyway, losing sight of the main street and having to look up to pinpoint my bearings. While I search for fluorescent showgirl signs and illuminated advertisements, I cannot help but think of my daughter. Jessica had become a completely different person in Khristoff's household. She had given up her life in virtue for a chance at disgraceful power, and now she is clueless and unrelenting to the man who saved her life.

The red show lights of an adult venue illuminate the walkway. As I pass, I notice a female dancer who tries to lure me in. She uses gyrating hips and provocative thrusts of her upper torso, caressing her barely covered body with promiscuous ideas of pleasure. Stopping for a smiling stare and an exchange of winks, I sense the impulse to indulge.

Her single labret piercing against her petite face glistens against the light of her stage, symbolizing the slightest hardened edge in her personality. Her long brown hair is tied in twin braids with strands of fiber optics rotating in colors. Beads of sweat appear on her flat stomach, illustrating the workout she is willing to endure. She twists her hips and waives her wrists, swinging her hair from side to side. If I could be on the other side of the glass, I would hear the music and rhythm she uses in her nightly routine.

The saliva in my mouth begins to saturate my tongue but I shake my head out of the trance and remember my path and the outcome of my journey. I must hold on to the strength I received from all those who believe in me. A voice speaks from the depths of my heart, and it recites a verse from a religion that starts to make sense.

I have come to understand that no temptation has overtaken me except what is common to mankind. And the Father is faithful. He will not let me be tempted beyond what I can bear. But when I am tempted, he will also provide a way out so that I can endure it.

"You don't worry about anything, do you?" I tilt my head as I watch her dance.

"I wouldn't say that." A voice startles me into seeing my staring reflection in the glass that separates me from the dancer.

"She has everything she needs." I glance at the man next to me but return my focus forward.

"Probably not --" The short man steps closer into the light of the projected venue and smiles, which excites the girl. "-- but she looks old enough to be in there."

I cannot help but think that I am in a dream, being tested against the morals of the right path. The dancer who stares down at me looks old enough to know what she is doing. From a distance, I should realize that she is a woman. She looks old enough to know what she wants, yet up close, she is probably younger than I expect. She could easily satisfy a man's lust for youth, but she makes me think only of the disappointment her parents must have felt when they discovered what their daughter had become.

"Did you come here for me? Or somebody's daughter?" I assume with a simple grin, looking up at the young woman.

"We've been looking for you."

"We?" I look around but see no other person standing on the street. "What do we want now?"

"Just information." He turns away from me and looks up at the dancing woman behind a thick layer of clear glass. She peels back the thin fabric of her bikini top that separates us from her birthday suit. "Where have you been these past couple days?"

"Doesn't matter," I cross my arms, turning to lean against the glass display, willing to stay silent while ignoring the free preview.

"It should." He moves closer to the soundproof glass. "You're taking things that don't belong to you," he flashes three fingers, rousing the woman's attention.

"Why would I do that?"

"Sunder," he looks at me. "I don't like being driven for no reason." He gestures to the shadows behind him, waving to the presence of someone I cannot see. "My orders are to bring you in for questioning."

The seriousness in his Hispanic accent plays with my memory. I remember the marketplace's mob mentality. The loophole that ended Uni's life, and I find myself in the presence of the only person who has seen me cry.

From the alleyway across the street, a couple of large men emerge from the shadows. They step into the show lights of the woman's advertisement window. I can see that they are wearing desert suits, heavy boots, neuro-metal gloves, and illuminated gas masks.

"What do you want from me?" I look over the other two Collars who have their arms crossed. "Why can't you just leave me alone?"

"I'd stop talking if I were you," the Collar with the Hispanic accent approaches me as I back up into the other two men.

"Why? So Mr. Big Arms and Tiny Head here can rough me up more than your fat tongue?"

"You'll address me as Sergeant Valdez." He starts

walking, forcing me to join his direction with a push of my shoulder.

The further away from the show lights we travel, the darker the streets of Thicket become. The streets are empty, but the alleyways are starting to swell with pedestrians looking for another late-night business to occupy. We four men merge with a group of people who look to be headed in the same direction.

I watch as boys and girls laugh in procession, sliding glances at us as we all walk together. I turn to Valdez who keeps a straight face through the entire march.

"If you found what you think I stole, would you let me go?"

Valdez stops walking and turns back to me.

"What makes you think I'll believe you?" He picks at my desert suit. "You've been outside too long."
"What if I can get you the thief?" I want to follow up with a riddle such as what one gets when crossing a Collar and a bulb of cauliflower, but I feel silenced in their forward stares.
"Where?" He glares with unimpressed eyes.
"The East Sector Club."
"Right," Valdez starts laughing.
"What?" I frown, unwilling to understand the joke.
"If that's your last request, I'll give that to you."
"I'm serious!"
"Sure, you are," he gestures for the other two agents to push me forward, forcing me to lead the way.

We walk through alleyways of steam vent exhaust pipes. When I notice the illuminated sign and line of waiting party goers, I recognize the entry-port to the East Sector Club.

"I don't think we'll be able to get in." I sound like a pessimist, slowing my footsteps on our way to the entry-port.

"We won't have any trouble." Valdez keeps his focus forward, moving me along.

The large man standing outside the club's entry-port seems larger than before. Valdez walks up to the bouncer and shakes his hand, exchanging words that I am not able to understand. The bouncer looks me over, and with a smile in remembering the other night, lets us enter without a second guess.

Inside the East Sector Club, I gaze over the league of dancing heads. The disco lights and laser shows are still set in motion. Stars and circles reflect off mirrored surfaces and the Silver Collars around the three men who escort me across the illuminated dance floor.

One of the masked men escorting me points to the back of the club. Valdez acknowledges with an upward nod. My imagination wanders through the crowd, searching for the hunched stature of Khristoff, who I believe would have disguised himself as one of the dancers. I feel the need to see him now, more than ever.

"You have ten minutes." Valdez speaks into my ear.

Valdez snaps his fingers which can barely be heard with the loud music overhead. I am pushed forward, left to wander the club without supervision.

I blink in succession, remembering the events of Khristoff's demise. I picture the powerful aura that surrounded his neuro-metal body only seconds before the comp-ucube began to smoke. I remember the way the surface of the comp-ucube acted out against Khristoff's connected invasion.

I want to stop and think, but I feel rushed by the three men who stand between me and the entry-port. I imagine seeing Khristoff in the marketplace and the resulting screams of fear that would result in his mere presence. I start to remember meeting Khristoff inside the Suite Oasis with Shantelle.

My steps, like my mind, should never be confronted. I see Khristoff's face alongside Uni and his crazy charades of super salesmanship. The further I walk away from Valdez, the more strenuous my internal questions become. I wonder how a hunchback absconder would be able to move through the crowds of the marketplace without rousing suspicion. I ponder the origins of Khristoff's desert suit and the way he possibly entered the city undetected.

A large crowd of dancers occupies the center of the club, hindering a direct path to the other side. Slowly, as individuals drift past their partners in a chorus line of kicked up shins, I spot a couple of familiar faces. With no obstruction, I recognize Thumbs and Laci at their usual floating table surrounded by a group of eager faces.

The hovering table is illuminated with another holographic show of Thumbs and his exploits. Hands that pass through the floating image join in a Cau-li tab exchange, which is obvious to me, but perhaps not to everyone in the club.

I always believed that false accusations would lead to expressions of shock, so protocol tends to focus on the public entourage of all gritty dispositions. I remember how Thumbs treated me the first time we met and what first impression he left me to create. I laugh a little, finding the humor in leading authorities to his farmer's market.

"Digis?" Thumbs looks up from his conversation. "What are you doing here?"

I feel the urge to sit, but also hoping our conversation is brief. Recalling our first conversation, I fall back into old habits.

"I'm looking for a thief."
"Uh --" he chuckles, insulted by the game I am playing. "You still don't know who I am."

I picture Uni in the struggle of the marketplace with Laci's older sister in a pool of her own blood. I remember Laci screaming for help and Thumbs being in the clutches of a maddening adult. Uni mentioned that he was trying to prevent another uprising and that Thumbs was responsible for starting the revolution.

Uni wanted to prevent Thumbs from killing everyone.

"Why Uni?" I stare at Thumbs through the holographic image on the table.

"Uni? You mean the crazy rat? He was asking too many questions." Thumbs smiles at a girl who accepts a dosage of Cau-li from him. "I've got a reputation to adhere to."

"So, you let Anneli die?" I look at Laci who keeps her face hidden from the light.

"Collateral." Thumbs presses a few buttons on his comp-uzync, erasing the holographic image from view. "Just like the priest." His attention becomes scattered among program windows littering the table's digital display. "We can't hold on to everyone."

I think about Uni, who died because of the city's need for justice and vengeance. Khristoff, who died because of his arrogance and greed. Then I picture Miko in the Medic Tower, recovering from the wounds that now make sense.

"Let me ask you something, Sunny." Thumbs leans forward on the table. "Do you believe me because he tried to kill me?"

I want to lie but find no use in denying what I originally thought. Loy did not die before becoming the monster within.

"Or because of my ability to tell you the truth." Thumbs leans in closer so only I can hear. "And I have to thank you. I wouldn't have been able to get this far without your gullible sense of family values."

The hate and confusion begin to mix in the pit of my stomach. I did not know that Shantelle would mislead me from the start, nor did I want to believe that she was being manipulated by so many of her friends. I remember the way she clung to her oblivious nature, recalling nothing of our history together.

"If I knew how easy it was to erase Shantelle, she wouldn't have met you and she wouldn't be broken." Thumbs smiles, showing me his interpretation of being disappointed. "Too bad." He leans back, ignoring me, and tucks a lock of Laci's hair behind her ear.

I feel as if I have heard enough. Thumbs has threatened my life and the life of my daughter for the sake of the comp-ucube. An innocent man has been judged based on the lies fabricated in this youth's name. A priest is in the hospital for trying to reach out to those who would be the future of our city, and everything now rests on the shoulders of a boy who the people of Thicket know as Thumbs. He may identify himself as someone in charge, but I still see him as the arrogant child who claims to know how everything works.

I crawl over the floating table, lunging at him. My hands reach his neck, imagining the power that Uni once felt. Just as my fingers process the fabric of his desert suit, the two masked Collars grab me by the arms and drag me back.

"Hey!" Valdez moves to help hold me still, standing between me and Thumbs. "What are you doing?"

245

"He's been lying from the beginning!" I try to break free. "He's going to kill everyone!"

"That's right, Digis." Thumbs sits back in his chair once he is sure that the Collars have me contained. "You can't hurt the main investment." He points to his own forehead. "Think about it."

"Val!" I look to the short sergeant. "That's your thief! You got to believe me! He knows too much about SCS! If you let him go, he'll take over the city!"

"This guy's harassing us!" Thumbs points at me as if ordering the two masked Collars to haul me out of the club.

I reach out for Thumbs and grab a lock of his hair, tearing a few strands from his scalp. The dramatic performance of his high-pitched scream is well received by the group surrounding us. The two men pull me back.

"Orders, sir?" One Collar turns to their sergeant.

Valdez looks back at me, believing that I am ready for a fight.

"Take him to the holding tower."
"Wait!" Thumbs interrupts.
"Excuse me?" Valdez raises an eyebrow.
"Take him to the city's entry-port." He speaks with a sinister smile that seems too mature for his age. "Let the desert have him. He doesn't deserve to be here."

Sergeant Valdez unlocks his comp-uzync and accesses the SCS mainframe through a series of input commands and hand gestures. He connects to

Headquarters and mumbles in the microphone. A moment passes and his orders appear in the comp-uzync screen.

The order to bring me in for questioning turns into disposing of me in the desert. As if settling some debt with my authority, Valdez accepts the new order from Headquarters without hesitation.

"What a coincidence." Valdez mumbles as he escorts me toward the club's exit.

Thumbs rises from his seat and runs around the table, acting out his excitement about my banishment. Feeling compelled to venture along, he follows us toward the club's entry-port. Laci reaches out to Thumbs before he gets too far from the suspended table.

"You shouldn't have done that." She looks in his eyes with a glimmer of sympathy.

"I'm not doing anything." Thumbs rips his arm free of her clutches. "I'm watching it all happen. This is better than UD vision."

"Don't you remember what Sunny did for you in the marketplace?" Laci glances at her comp-uzync and the digital prints of her sister. "He saved your life and this is how you're going to repay him?"

"Well, he deserves it!" He seems to be running short on excuses by the way he rips Laci's Imprint Drive from her comp-uzync. "We have to clean up his mess. Shantelle should have just taken the cube when she had the chance. If it wasn't for that damn priest, she'd still remember what to do. It's all her fault!"

Sergeant Valdez and I, escorted by the grips of two Collars, reach the other side of the loud dance club.

Intimidated by Thumbs, Laci deflects his smile with a frown, rejecting his attempt to overrun her with guilt. She turns in her seat, brushing him off with her cold shoulder.

Near the front of the club, Sergeant Valdez pushes me through the crowd. He does not look to be in the best mood, even while following orders to lead his prisoner toward their immediate punishment.

"Val! You know you can't do this to me!" I try again to break free but succumb to the tight hold of the two large men. "I can get you the cube."

"Your ten minutes are up, Sunder." Valdez tries to hide his compassion.

"You're too slow, Sunny." Thumbs interrupts, joining the group as we pass the bouncer outside. "You need to learn how to lead."

The outside of the club is busier as the night draws in more people. The lights that play in the steam vent puddles reflect me in a prisoner's hold. Thumbs has to walk twice as fast to keep pace with our long strides. The two masked Collars remain quiet while they walk, and Valdez glances at Thumbs as we pass an intersecting alleyway.

"This doesn't concern you." He tries to persuade Thumbs to leave.

"Yes, it does!"

"Uni should have strangled you," I mumble.

"What's that, Sunny?" Thumbs catches up with a cupped hand around his ear. "Are you threatening me? You need to learn to not let your emotions get involved." He drops his hand in a hysterical laugh, hitting the short Hispanic in his shoulder for comical support. "Am I right?"

"If you touch me again, I'll place you under arrest."

The further along we all walk, the deeper in thought I sink. As we pass through the northern edge of the marketplace, I think about Arlita and her weekly forecasts on my mundane life. Passing between the Medical Wings, I think about Miko and the strength religion used to give me when I struggled in doubt. These days I feel as though I am drowning, and I remember that a lifeguard is meant to walk on water. I think about my wife and the way she lived without a proper husband to hold her at night. I also reminisce on Jessica and the day that I had to leave them both. It is this memory that gives me an idea.

"Sergeant!" I try again to reason with the Silver Collar agent. "This kid has the comp-ucube. He's taking over SCS!"

"No, I'm not!" Thumbs sounds defensive. "Don't blame me for what you're trying to do!"

"Sergeant! This kid has the cube!" I try my luck at assuming. "Check his pockets."

"You're a liar!" Thumbs points his finger.

Valdez glares at me with a pessimistic expression. He glances at Thumbs and quickly makes a decision. He approaches the young absconder.

249

"Empty your pockets."
"I don't consent."

Valdez gestures to the two masked men. Less than a hundred yards from the wasteland entry-port, they grab Thumbs by the arms and hold him still. He tries to kick and scream but his mouth is muffled, restrained by one of their large hands.

After patting the boy's desert suit, Sergeant Valdez exhales in disappointment. He pulls a handful of C-Tabs, several nicotine discs, a Silver Collar and the comp-ucube from a zippered pocket. He holds up the cube for Thumbs to explain.

"Does this belong to you?"
"It's my right!" Thumbs shouts over him.
"What about your suit? You steal that too?" Valdez nods at the two men.

The two masked men tighten their grip around the young absconder, showing confidence that they have the correct prisoner.

"That cube is too powerful for any one person to possess." I watch Valdez turn the device over.
"It should never have left us in the first place," Valdez glances at me as he studies the object's identifiable marks. "So, I can either trust you," he pauses, gently scratching his face. "Or deal with you."
"Let me talk to him." I take a step toward the two masked men holding Thumbs.

Valdez smiles as he hands me an egg-shaped device, seeing the irony in the situation. The two Collars release the young absconder's arms and push him near the wall, close to the wasteland entry-port where he could be watched as I speak.

"You know, Thumbs," I approach with a cheerful tone, keeping the volume of my voice to a minimum. "There are many reasons for failure in this world, but not a single excuse."

"I didn't fail! Your family failed!" Thumbs moves away from the wall, trying to intimidate me.

"Nobody here wants to see this world fall into another great catastrophe. Someone close told me once to follow the willow. At the time, I didn't know what she meant. That is, until I heard the hysterical rants of a mother at the top of the cathedral steps. Her sins had gotten the best of her. I simply won't allow your sins to infect the rest of this peaceful city." I put my hands in my pockets and turn back to Sergeant Valdez with a smile. "I have to admit, I thought it would be me hearing this speech."

"I'm not falling for that." Thumbs looks me over.

"Do I lie?" I breathe in deep, glancing down at the dirt on my boots. "Tell me, Thumbs. Do you know the tale of the man who tried to live forever?"

"Yeah, what about him?"

"Have you ever seen a bat savagely devour another bat?"

"I know where this is going, and I've heard it all before."

I walk up to the entry-port and pull on a large lever

near the circular entryway. Twisting gears and harmonious chirps of electricity resonate from within the walls of reseeded steel. The outside air that seeps into the city smells burnt. What I remember as an endless desert of unbelievable sandstorms, crashing into one another like tornadoes of dirt and grime, is now a way for me to transition my days.

"I'll give you a chance." I reveal the rooting device. "But you can never return."

"Are you dumb?" Thumbs drops his jaw. "Are you going to lock me out?" He tries to smile his way into rejecting the agreement.

"Something like that."

"People will know my sacrifice is just another way for SCS to control them," he looks around at the people who have gathered near the wasteland entry-port.

"Then we're even."

"You think that thing is going to work on me?" He tries to laugh. "I can't be put to sleep."

"If you want my opinion, I'd disappear," I quickly glance at the horizon. "Just go."

"This is all you can do? You never wore a Collar, and you will never control me." His voice deepens as if the point he is trying to make is to be recorded for future generations.

"Of course not."

"Don't think you can intimidate me." He stares at me with widened eyes that seem to be getting brighter.

"Then don't get stepped on." I attach the rooter to his comp-uzync.

The gears inside the egg-shaped device loudly crank

against the software of his comp-uzync. His sight will darken, leaving him with a sinking feeling in his body, as if he is slowly submerged into an abyss of soothing shadows. I imagine Thumbs to be on the verge of losing consciousness, but in a moment of benign brilliance, he grabs his implant. Disregarding the rooting process, he removes his comp-uzync, leaving an empty cavity for his implant. His eyes roll forward as he catches his breath.

"Good luck finding it."

I pull the comp-uzync from his grip and notice that his Imprint Drive is no longer access ready. Such as rebooting a computer during a critical update, Thumbs is making sure the Silver Collar Society has nothing to show for harassing him.

The entry-port's gears twist in loud cranks as the entryway slowly closes, leaving me and the other three Collars in the comforting arms of the city of Thicket. The inner and outer shell of Thicket's wall prevents anyone from simply gaining access. As Thumbs stands on the other side of the sealed entry-port, I try not to calculate his chances of survival. I try to imagine that as an example of his humility, he sprints away crying.

"I would remember for future reference," Valdez pulls me away from the other men. "We can't have this kind of thing happen again."

"Don't trust absconders, got it." I make my point with a nod.

"Don't get cute, Sunder." His face turns serious. "I'm doing you a favor. Remember that."

Sergeant Valdez glares me over as I return the rooter and uprooted comp-uzync unit with a dumbstruck look. He gestures for the other Collars to follow him.

"You know, he can't get back in." I try to assure him.

As quickly as they turn their backs on me, they disappear into the darkness. Soon I am standing near the shadows with the light of a nearby glass advertisement board reflecting off my mimicking comp-uzync.

"I have to ask you." Shantelle slowly appears from the darkness. "Did you love my mother?"

I try my best to hold back a smile, forcing my focus to answer in a serious tone.

"More than the space between the stars."
"Do you know what happened to her?" She walks closer to me, showing signs that she is expecting to be hugged.
"I don't," I sigh.

I wish I could say more. I wish I could say that I helped Sherianne escape the confines of the city. I wish I could say that I returned to the absconder camp to check on my family and that I saw the signs that could have prevented their demise.

"Did you draw this?" Shantelle pulls the drawing from her front pocket and holds it near her waist. "She looks so happy."

I start to wonder if Shantelle's memory has returned or if she is trying to regain my trust by making me answer her questions correctly. I wish I knew what happened to Sherianne. I wish the relationship between me and my daughter could be normal, but as I glance around, reality snaps me back into place and I must remember that things are this way for a reason beyond our control. Not even God knows our path. God only knows the trials we face and the decisions we make.

"A part of me wants to believe that you could be my father." She looks up at me with tears in her eyes. "I cycle through so many identities, the family I had is forever gone. I would give anything to feel that security again."

"Shantelle, I --"

"Just tell me something," she interrupts. "I know you're a father to some kid out there. If they did something horrible to you, could you ever forgive them?"

"I can't tell you that I'll forget what you did."

Shantelle lowers her head in shame, letting a tear fall to the neuro-metal pavement below. I feel the guilt she puts out like a radiator of heat that is responsible for the mess we are both in. She knows the consequences of her actions and the ramifications with the Silver Collar Society.

"But I can tell you this." I slowly approach her. "I'll always forgive you." I open my arms, inviting her in for a friendly embrace.

255

Her warmth cradles me like I have always wanted. For one solid moment, I feel united with both Sherianne and the daughter I never got to raise. As I stare at the top of her head, an idea crosses my mind that could settle most of our problems.

"Tomorrow," I hold her by her shoulders to look in her eyes. "We'll talk with citizen registration. We'll let the city office know that I'm adopting you."

Shantelle's eyes light up with an outcry of emotions.

"Then we can be a family again, and we won't have to worry about anyone taking you away from me."

Shantelle's smile looks exactly like Sherianne. As we embrace for a hug, I stare at the sealed entry-port and think about Thumbs.

Gaining distance from Thicket, Thumbs refuses to stop as he runs toward the nearest absconder camp. The arrogance coursing through his veins intensifies with the anticipation of what he will find. He remembers the story of the man who tried to live forever, relating to the pain of being abandoned.

He remembers the caves that he explored as a child and the shovels he used to carry the bat carcasses back to the processing bins. He remembers scavenging the land with Anneli and Laci outside the absconder camp, avoiding the adults in preparation of the Collar's arrival.

The defectors of the absconder camp were subjected to experimental effects. Although their symptoms mimicked those of basic memory loss, Shantelle and Sherianne were among those contained and exposed to the lingering disease of Willow Amnesia.

Thumbs thinks on Shantelle's state of mind and her chances of having a normal life. Irritated by the thought of her happiness, he picks up a rock and launches it at a scurrying Hyltot. He pictures the neuro-metal skin that protected his Father's body from the elements of the wasteland.

Thumbs smiles at the crushed body of the bleeding Hyltot, imagining his revenge on my treachery and wrongdoing. He stares at a series of clouds that begin to form on the horizon, adamant on surviving longer than the reign of the immortal man.

Chapter 15

Recycled Wire

..

"Now the Spirit expressly says that in later times some
will depart from the faith by devoting themselves to
deceitful spirits and teachings of demons."

1 Timothy 4:1

..

The mornings in Thicket are always a sight to
behold. Mixing in with the atmosphere of the dead
landscape, the brilliant lives of the dawn create a
breathtaking view from any tall building in the city.
From the street level, the colors of the morning sunrise
reflect off the link-rail tubes and the towers of reseeded
steel. The crackling sounds beyond the city's borders
are the easiest to hear during the early hours of silence
before most of the population take to the streets.

A rumor in Thicket spreads quicker than wildfire so
I am not surprised to hear what has happened to
Thumbs from the people in the marketplace. People on
the streets share in the gossip while vendors embellish
the same stories with their sales. A rumor that begins
near the boundary's entry-port will make its way
through the alleyways of the homeless, between the
dancers of the East Sector Club who will share the
information with friends, across the link-rail system by
interactive strangers, and over the neuro-metal
pavement to Arlita's apartment.

"No doubt you've heard the same news." Arlita
unclasps her hands, placing them on the table before

her.

I sit back in my chair with my elbows stretched out and fingers interlocked behind my neck. My eyes survey the apartment that has come to be my second home. At the sight of a manufactured mobile that hangs with adorned gadgets of the old world, I feel reminded of a time not yet under full control of its electronic appendages. Marveling over Arlita's collection of aluminum cans, each dressed in unique fonts and colors of companies that no longer exist, I wonder how people ever survived on such malnourished liquids.

"I have," my voice cracks. "But I don't believe a word of it."

"The people are talking." Arlita rises from her seat and approaches a hydro-generator that works as a heated purifier, emitting steam from its top opening. "They're saying you're a hero."

"For what?" I lift my right foot and cross my leg, resting my heavy ankle on my knee. "Sending a kid to the wasteland? Doing the duty of a Collar? I feel right at home with those leaders in that book of yours." I hold on to my shin, stretching my back and breathing in the smell of Arlita's apartment.

"You can't blame yourself for the boy's fate. It was the path of corruption he chose." She takes a sip from a mug that looks molded from the wet earth. "Besides, what do you think would've happened if you just went home?"

I look at the ceiling, thinking on the people whose comp-uzyncs are connected to the mainframe

259

indefinitely, on behalf of the religious connection they all hoped to make. I try to imagine the daunting effect on the entire population. I ponder the scenario of thousands of absconders roaming the streets at the command of a teenage boy. I visualize the destruction of upper-class buildings at the expense of proving a point. I massage the back of my neck, cracking a smile.

"I guess we'd all be drinking gasoline." My rubbing turns into scratching. "But if it happens again, I won't have to run."

"It's been a few days now. How's the new leg?" Arlita leans to the side, trying to see my leg from a different angle.

I slap my shin, creating a hollow bang that seems to echo in the apartment.

"The best they could offer me was a free upgrade." I lift the fabric covering my shin, exposing an artificial limb, cast from neuro-metal and Silver. Connected to my femur, I show Arlita my newest norm.

"Since I did so much for them --" I want to say more but I stop, thinking on the memory of Uni and the order given to end his life. I drop my foot in a heavy fall and stand to approach a cluttered shelf. I pick up a shiny object as if I am shopping for another trinket. "Things won't be the same."

"I can agree with you there." Arlita takes another sip of hot water. "What became of the cube?"

"The cube?" My focus breaks as I turn to answer. "SCS had it dismantled." I turn back to the shelf and pick up a spherical object that contains a clear liquid and a storm of white flakes over a city scene. "At least that's what they told me." I shake the globe and the flakes swirl around the miniature buildings. "Aren't these buildings already underwater?"

Arlita spits up a little water as she tries to drink, smiling at my ignorance and trying not to laugh. I place the snow globe on the shelf, along with the display of twentieth century artifacts that remind me of my daughter's curiosity. I remember when she was young and had a new set of eyes in the world, holding on to my forefinger before she could speak or ask about the world.

"I don't know if she'll ever remember." I watch the snowflakes settle.

"Who do you mean?" Arlita sets her cup down.

"Jessica. She still doesn't recognize me." I place a hand on the shelf, hanging my face in embarrassment.

"Well, some things are hard to process." She taps the outside of her cup and raises her eyebrows, staring into the distance. "Sometimes, a little courage is all you need to let go."

"As always, Lita, you know just what to say. But I can't help but think that Thumbs had something to do with it." I slump back to the empty seat across from her.

"With your daughter?"

"Yeah." I lean forward in the chair, laying my arms on the table. "When I was at the East Sector Club, the atmosphere was --" I pause, thinking of the way people responded to the Collar in the club. "-- different."

"How do you mean?" She tilts her head back, slurping the last of her water.

"The air –" I tally my fingers. "-- the people -- the dancing -- the music – the light seemed out of sync. It was almost as if everything was programmed to fit someone's impulse. I mean I have no basis for reference, but it felt like Thumbs was able to use the cube before SCS took it back."

"But if that were true, he could have done a lot more. He would have had people there to protect him."

"It's weird. Those Collars didn't care about him at first. It was like he was invisible."

"Why would they ignore him?"

"Exactly." I raise my eyebrows, pointing a finger at her. "They had to have seen what he was doing."

"He wasn't hiding, was he?" She waves her hand in the air, as if helping to move along her train of thoughts. "I mean, any suspicion would lead you to at least question him, right?"

"Right," I stare off in the distance. "Except --"

I think about the communications system backing the city of Thicket. The entire relay of wireless information is vital to the success of the Silver Collar Society. When a creature like Khristoff is capable of interfering with the direct orders of a Silver Collar agent, the simplest of situations become jeopardized. Thumbs may have been given the same access, the same power to fake complete control, if only to dispose of his own adversary.

"It was like he was granted a free pass with access to our database."

"The cube gave him access? How?" Arlita squints, unsure of how I will answer.

"Code words -- secret channels -- legal immunity --

262

I don't really know." I raise my elbows on the table to rub the top of my head. "You don't think Willow Amnesia has anything to do with it, do you?"

"Should it?" Arlita looks confused, standing to carry her cup to the hydro-generator.

"I don't know," my head falls back. "I guess it doesn't really matter. His body is probably somewhere between Thicket and Crowchest."

"I need to tell you something," Arlita turns. "Promise you won't get mad."

"What is it?" My smirk drops to a serious look of puzzlement.

"I tapped into SCS security."

"Really?" I chuckle. "Aren't you paranoid enough?"

"Well, I heard about a break-in at the Oasis." She returns to the table and places her fingernails into the cracks of the orb that sits between us. "Let me --" she pauses, squinting at the foggy complexion. "Show you what I found."

The glass orb flickers in shades of blue and green, focusing its resolution on a clear image of the Suite Oasis. A clearly defined person, dressed in a long dark robe with a deep hood, paces the room that is still littered with mechanical parts. The security feed captures the individual throwing tools and punching a holding tank, overturning a collection bin. With each punch that lands against a metallic surface, sparks fly into the air like a shower of electricity.

The figure's long robe sways in the motion of each aggressive footstep. The gaps in the fabric reveal a darkened skin tone that resembles the tar-like surface of neuro-metal. Cracks separate wrists from arms and ankles from legs in the same pattern as Khristoff's body.

"And?" I blink. "Khristoff was angry. He's still dead."

"This is yesterday."

"That's impossible." I stare at the glass orb that is now zoomed in on the dark figure. "His body was a melted shell when I left."

"Are you sure?" Arlita manipulates the orb by twisting the cracks with her fingernails. "I checked the other recordings and couldn't find his body."

"He couldn't have survived --" I almost choke on my disbelief, breaking my voice.

The short figure in the video footage raises a hand to his hood and pulls back on the fabric. His bald head is coated in a thick layer of neuro-metal with cracks along the major segments of his skull, but the back part of his head is missing, with only pieces of recycled wire used to fill in the shape. His eyes are a glowing yellow and orange, and his mouth is sealed shut. He reaches into his pocket and reveals an object I can barely see without squinting into the viewing orb.

"What is that?"

The object is inserted into a newly implanted comp-uzync. The tiny room becomes illuminated by a holographic image of the comp-ucube's digital schematics. The dark figure turns to the security camera with eyes full of electricity, overloading the camera feed and melting the lens.

The fate of Thicket rests in the hands of one man.

As a not-for-profit publisher, Arkermin Project is dedicated to making available works of literature for the benefit of all mankind. We publish works including, but not limited to, translations of future predictions and conspiracy theories, historical crossovers, fiendish foreign fables, religious spirituality, apocalyptic survival guides, and boundless erotica. We publish our titles with the appreciation of the written word and with the art of storytelling. Let us publish your story today.

..

266

Made in the USA
Columbia, SC
17 May 2023

16875108R00169